I0780877

PRINCE EDWARD ISLAND

CAMDEN
MYSTERY CLUB

SEQUEL

ANNE HOTCHKIS

INK START MEDIA
265 Eastchester Dr Ste 133 #102
High Point NC 27262

TABLE OF CONTENTS

BOOK 4:

MYSTERY AT BEN'S LAKE

CHAPTER 1

"A murder mystery weekend would be great!" exclaimed Trish Camden as she spoke to the Camden Mystery Club. "I'm excited about our wilderness camping adventure at Ben's Lake this weekend planned by the manager of the Lake. The pandemic with all the COVID 19 restrictions has limited our involvement in group activities; however, I've been in contact with Cal Morgan, the owner at Ben's Lake and he assures me that all social distancing measures will be enforced and the murder mystery will be done in small groups. I told him we 're a group of five, which isn't a problem he says."

"It sounds like fun. Will we have to wear masks while we are there?" asked Josie.

"Not outside but if we are indoors or are within six feet of each other then we'll have to. We should come prepared with our masks to be on the safe side."

"Who's looking after the food for the activity?" asked Paul. "I'd be happy to take on this task."

The small club's members meeting in the basement of the Camden's home were in agreement that Paul take charge of the food, but said they'd be cooking on an open fire and they were leery of Paul's unhealthy food habits. "Don't forget to bring essentials like protein, carbs, and fruits and vegetables. We each need to bring our own water supply," said Charlie.

"Not a problem."

"When we get there, Cal will set us up with two canoes and direct us to the wilderness camping sites. The murder mystery will begin at 6:00 p.m. on Friday night starting at the main office where we will get our first clue," said Trish.

"This sounds very exciting," said John, Josie's twin. "We've never been on an actual murder mystery weekend. Will we need tents or are we going to make lean-tos?"

"The only thing I know we will have for our use is a grill and an outhouse. What does the club think about tents or lean-tos? The manager probably doesn't want us to cut down trees for a lean-to; so I suggest we bring a tent," said Charlie.

"We'll be responsible for our own drinks and we can use lake water to wash up camping dishes," said Trish.

The CMC finalized their plans and discussed how a fake murder mystery would take place at Ben's Lake. They departed enthusiastically from the meeting and made arrangements for Trish, Charlie and Paul to take the old Toyota while the twins would get a drive to the Lake with their mom. The club members thought this was a good way to end the summer before heading back to school. Who knew how the COVID restrictions would affect their school events?

Cal Morgan met the CMC members at the office Friday at 4:00 p.m. He signed them in and took them with all their gear to the two canoes they would need to paddle across the lake to the remote wilderness camping site. "Lay claim on any site you want as you are the earliest group to arrive," said Cal. "Meet back at the office at 6:00 p.m. for your first clue to the murder mystery weekend. The other groups will have to sign in and wait for their turn to explore the signs of the mystery, as only one group can follow the clues at a time. Your club will start. See you at 6:00 p.m."

The twins piled their gear and the six-man tent into one of the canoes with all the food Paul had brought. Charlie, Trish and Paul took their own backpacks and operated the second canoe. They paddled their way across the lake in a hot, August sun, allowing themselves to splash water at each other to feel some relief from the humidity. The forest was thick and they noticed primitive sites well- spaced apart from other ones. Once they banked the canoes, they decided on a site hidden from the openness of the campground across from the lake and pitched the tent. Paul suggested they eat sandwiches for supper, as it was too hot to cook anything. Everyone agreed; so Paul unpacked the food. By the time they had eaten, Trish was eager to start the murder mystery and checked her watch which said 5:30 p.m.

"We'd better take the canoes and head for the office. We are to be there by six," she said. The club agreed and they left their campsite and made their way to the office. They arrived right on schedule. Cal was there with his assistant, George Mason, his lazy business partner who made Cal's life miserable.

Cal gave Charlie a map of Ben's Lake and passed the first clue to Trish. "Good luck. You have two hours to find the murderer." Excitedly the CMC wanted to read the first clue.

CLUE #1

COVID 19 – Social distancing is essential.
Wash your hands please and thank you.

If not, you must go to prison. You cannot escape!

"What does that mean?" asked John. "We've heard all this before. There must be a hidden meaning in the message."

"Let's look at the map," said Charlie.

"What do the underlined letters mean? It could be some kind of code," said Trish. "Let's write out the letters that are underlined."

Calissenttoprison Trish printed on a piece of paper. "If we separate them into words, we have, Cal is sent to prison. Then the last line says 'You cannot escape!' Charlie, what does the map show?"

"I think I've got it! There is an Escape Room marked on the map. We are to go to the Escape Room," said Charlie.

"Way to go!" said Josie.

The CMC followed the map to the Escape Room. They opened the door with ease but as soon as they entered, the door locked behind them. This was unnerving and they felt fearful. They had one hour in the locked room to complete the clues. There was a small window allowing for some light to enter the room. The teens were amazed at the huge table in front of them. On the table was a large box. It was filled with puzzles, codes, and clues to find the key to unlock the door. The CMC had experience with codes and they solved the puzzles within thirty minutes. They found the key, unlocked the door and were once more out of the Escape Room, looking at the map and clue # 2 which they picked up when they found the key.

CLUE #2

Find out the Legend of the Black Hoodie Man. "Where do we start?" asked Paul.

"I bet some of the campers, especially the kids, might have this information. Let's go and ask some of them," said Trish. Trish led the way to the camper trailers and saw a couple of girls on a trampoline. "Hello. Do either of you know the story about the Black Hoodie Man?"

"Are you here for the murder mystery weekend?" asked one of the girls. "My name is Greta and my sister is Maggie; we've been told to tell you the story if you ask."

"Yes, we've just come out of the Escape Room and we have a clue to ask about the Legend of the Black Hoodie Man," said Charlie. "Can you girls help us?"

The girls embellished the story of the Black Hoodie Man. First, they explained that the Man in a black hooded jacket came out after dark and he carried a bloody knife and chased after boys and girls to kill them. "We are scared of the Black Hoodie Man. I saw a stranger once after dark and it looked just like the Black Hoodie Man," said the older girl, Maggie. "Our parents say it's not true but we think it is true."

"Now that you know the legend, you will get the third clue. Here it is." The girls jumped off the trampoline and passed the clue to the mystery club. "Stay safe."

CLUE # 3

Fish for your next clue.

The Camden Mystery Club was stumped with this clue, but not for long. They looked around the lake. Charlie spotted some fishing rods on the dock. "It looks as if we have to go fishing," he said; "let's head out to the end of the dock."

"There are only three rods here. I guess we'll have to take turns. Oh look, there is a can of worms right here. I guess we're in the right place. I wonder how long we'll have to fish," said Trish.

"Probably until one of us catches a fish," said John.

"I think Charlie and I will let you, Josie and Paul, do the fishing," said Trish.

"That's fine with me," said Paul as he picked up a rod and began baiting a hook.

The twins likewise baited their hooks and cast the lines into the water. It was a warm, summer evening and it took at least half an hour before John got a bite. He reeled in the fish. No sooner did he do that, there was Cal coming over with the next clue. "We catch and release here at Ben's Lake," said Cal; "there are only two more clues and you are on your way to completing the murder mystery. Here is clue number four."

CLUE #4

Find a rope dangling from a Hemlock tree. Tie it to the
tree, make a noose and return to your campsite.

"Who knows their tree types?" asked Josie; "I don't know what a Hemlock tree looks like."

"All we have to do is look for a tree that has a rope hanging from it," said John.

"Well, our two-hour window to find the victim of our murder mystery is just about up," said Trish; "let's follow the trail in the woods. It will eventually lead us back to our campsite and the Hemlock tree with the rope will probably be within sight."

The five mystery club members trudged along the trail which circled Ben's Lake. All at once they came across a big, old tree with a rope hanging down from it. "This must be it," said Paul. Quickly Paul and Charlie tied the rope to a solid branch and then they made a running knot to form a noose. The hangman's halter was set. The club left the noose and headed for their campsite. When they got there, they saw the fifth and final clue stapled to a spruce tree.

CLUE #5

Go back to the Hemlock tree.
Bring the victim back to the office.

Excitedly the group made their way back to the tree and found a dummy dangling from the tree with the noose around its neck. They loosened the knot and carried their trophy victim down the path leading around the lake and headed towards the office. George and Cal were waiting for them. They had another team getting ready for the murder mystery event to begin at

8:00 p.m. Cal met the CMC team and congratulated them on arriving back at the office within the two-hour allotment.

"We found the victim," the club announced.

"I must go and reset the murder mystery clues," said Cal. "The next team is already here and waiting for their turn. There will be three more groups tomorrow starting at 9:00 a.m. The team with the best time will be our murder mystery champions."

CHAPTER 2

The evening campfire set up by Cal when darkness fell over the campground was attended by the campers at the lake and the Camden Mystery Club was invited as well. Paul brought hotdogs and marshmallows but Cal told them it was against the coronavirus protocol to eat at a public campfire; so Paul left the treats for the CMC to eat at their own fire at another time. Once it got dark the ghost stories began. Landon, the fourteen-year-old brother of Greta and Maggie relished the retelling of the Black Hoodie man, scaring his sisters and brother Broon to death. Landon was hysterical over how much his sissy little sisters and eleven- year- old brother believed the made-up story. "The bloody knife found next to a bloody dead body," he exaggerated, as he told the story, had younger children afraid of the dark.

The second murder mystery team had from 8:00 to 10:00 p.m. to complete the clues and it was well after dark when they returned with the dummy but they made it within the two- hour allotment. Since Cal was at the campfire, the team reported to him there. The main office closed at 10:00 for the night. George always locked up before retiring to his trailer on the property.

Cal was an early riser and wanted to get the office by 7:00 a.m., as the next team was to start at 9:00 and he and Victor had to set up the clues. The office was usually locked but this morning the office wasn't. He thought to himself that George must have forgotten to lock the door and he was peeved over George's carelessness and lackadaisical attitude. But when he opened the door he was traumatized to see George lying in a distorted position in a pool of blood with a knife stuck in his heart. He knelt beside the body and checked for a pulse. There was none. George was dead. Cal was shaken but made the call to 911 immediately.

RCMP officers, Staff Sergeant Rob Camden, Sergeant Frank Brown and Corporal Kurt Lewis as well as the coroner, Mack Pathius, arrived within the hour. The EMS arrived as well. Cal cancelled the remaining murder mystery activities for the day.

Victor and Lily MacEwen, the married couple whose four children spend their days at the Lake, lived in the house across from the office, and came over to see what was happening when they saw the police car and EMS van arrive. Victor was the handyman at the Lake and helped Cal with many chores while Lily looked after cleaning the washrooms. The agreement was that they could live rent -free for the summer months if they pitched in with campground maintenance.

"What's going on here?" asked Victor.

"There's been a murder," said Cal. "George is dead. I've cancelled the remaining murder mystery activities scheduled for the day. The police detectives are here to investigate the death."

Trish was scouring a pot on the other side of the lake from where she could see the RCMP car and EMS vehicle at the entrance to the park. She immediately raced back to the campsite to inform the club that something fishy was going on over at the office. Charlie, John, Josie, and Paul, the members of the Camden Mystery Club, were all curious to find out details. Paul had a pair of binoculars; so he went to the water's edge and tried to see if he could recognize faces of the police. The commotion at the office was too distant from the other side of the lake; so the whole club got into the canoes which they had taken back to their wilderness site after the bonfire last night and headed for the opposite shore.

Cal came over to speak with them. "George has been murdered," he said.

"Which detectives are here? Is our dad here?" piped up Trish.

"Who's your father?" asked Cal.

"RCMP Staff Sergeant for all of PEI, Rob Camden," said Trish.

"I don't know your father but there are three detectives as well as a coroner with a name badge labelled Dr. Mack Pathius in the office with the body. No one is allowed in there and they have cordoned off the office area. I know they will be looking for suspects at some point. I guess the team that did the murder mystery after your team will need to be brought in to be interviewed. The teams scheduled for today have been cancelled. Your team had the best time overall; so your team won the weekend murder mystery. It doesn't matter much anymore. George and I had our problems and he wasn't honest but I didn't wish him dead."

Greta and Maggie looked for breakfast and then came outside to see what was going on at the office. Landon, the eldest at 14 was followed by Maggie, 13, Greta, 12, and Broon, 11, who wore shorts and a T-shirt from last night's campfire. They sat on the veranda of the house not knowing what was happening. Lily came over and shooed the children into the house. "It's none of your business what's going on at the office. Help yourselves to cereal and toast and stay inside until the cops and EMS vehicle leave."

"But Ma, I want to know what's happening," said Landon indignantly. "You can't keep me inside. I'll find out what's happening with some of those teenagers out there." He shoved his way out the door before his mom could stop him. "What happened?" he asked.

"There's been a murder," said Trish. "The detectives and coroner are in the office with the body."

"Geez, who died?"

"His name is George. That's all I know for now," said Trish. "You live here at the Lake with your family? I saw you last night scaring the campers with the story of the Black Hoodie man. Well, the death may have occurred last night while everyone was at the campfire."

"Oh no. Not George, not George," cried Landon.

Victor approached his son to console him. "It's going to be okay, Landon. I know you and George had a special relationship. Things have a way of working their way out. You'll see. There is nothing you can do here. Why don't you go over to the house and have something to eat."

"Leave me alone, Dad. You don't understand, so buzz off."

Sergeant Frank Brown and Corporal Kurt Lewis assisted Dr. Mack Pathius in the office with the body. Rob Camden came to the Lake to check on his own kids. He knew the detectives were competent in searching for clues. When he saw the mystery club pulling up in canoes, he was relieved. Pathius said, "It appears to me that this stabbing occurred with the killer stabbing the heart of the man from a frontal position causing an instant death. There is no sign of a struggle. The time of death was approximately 11:00 p.m. last night. It looks as if you detectives have some work to do. I'll take the body back to the lab in the EMS vehicle for further analysis."

CHAPTER 3

Jessy Baird was having her morning coffee on her patio in Charlottetown when she got a text from her friend, Lily MacEwen. *George Mason is dead. Cops are here. He was murdered.* Jessy was pleased to hear the good news. *Now Cal will be able to have a normal job running the Lake,* she thought. She knew the stress George had caused Cal. Binge drinking, gambling, drugs on the premises, dealing with users coming to Ben's Lake for a fix, stealing from the cash box, and never lifting a finger to help as a business manager. Why Cal never fired him she didn't know but now he was dead. Good. Someone got to him and she knew it wasn't her boyfriend, Cal. Jessy was planning to go out to the Lake this afternoon. She decided to text Cal. *I heard the news. Do you want me to come to the Lake this pm?* Her text back from Cal said, *the detectives are taking statements from the campers. They should be done by noon. Please come this pm.*

I'll be there around 2 pm, she texted back.

CHAPTER 4

Two weeks earlier

Landon liked to hang around the office where forty- year-old George Mason sat outside puffing on a cigarette, reading a horse-racing magazine. "You ever been to the horse races, Landon?"

"No."

"I will take you sometime if you want, that is, if your old man will let you."

"Yeah, that would be cool."

George had his eye on Landon as a potential customer. He knew Landon would be gullible and naïve. He'd show him a thing or two, help him mature in the ways of the underworld. The horse races were scheduled for Saturday night in Charlottetown and with Victor's approval, Landon was allowed to accompany George to the races. Victor informed Landon to be wary and alert to any gambling that George might involve himself in.

Landon was innocent and trusting. He wanted to get away from his parents and siblings for a night. It was settled. George drove Landon in his beat-up old truck to the racetrack at 6 p.m., offering him a beer on the way into town. Landon took the opportunity to prove he was capable of whatever George put before him. He gulped the beer and pretended he was so cool.

Once they arrived at the track George Mason said, "I'll buy a guide to tonight's races and then I'll help you pick your horses to bet. I'll buy your first ticket. After that if you win you'll have to pay me for any other race you want me to bet on for you. You are not old enough to place a bet yourself. Here, have another beer. I've got a stash with us." George opened up his coat and displayed his pockets full of beer. Then he showed Landon his tote bag which was full of alcohol. Landon was starting to feel the effects of the beer. George explained the race guide book and Landon picked the horse he wanted to bet on. Mason placed Landon's first bet to win at the ticket booth. He placed his own bet on another horse to win, place or show.

"Hey, George, you brought the kid you've been talking about," said Mombo.

"Yeah, he's easy to fool."

"Come on over. I'd like you to meet him."

George had the two tickets and Mombo followed him back to the stands where Landon was nursing a second beer. "Landon, this is Mombo Katumba, a friend."

Mombo was a 40ish heavy-set wrestler type, with tattoos on both arms and a colourful pony tail with a half-shaved head and a beard. Landon had never met someone so rough looking but he trusted George; so he just said, "Hey."

"Here's your ticket on Fancy Pants to win. The odds are against him but stranger things have happened. Mombo, do you want a beer?"

"I brought my own."

"The horses are lining up for the first race. Landon, here is your ticket. Good luck."

George had a safe bet on Serenity to win, place, or show but Landon wanted to place his bet to win on Fancy Pants which was a long shot.

The horses were off. The announcer gave a full commentary of the race as the sulky drivers came around the track. Serenity was coming up on the inside while Fancy Pants was coming up on the outside. Landon, feeling a little buzz from the beer, cheered for his horse. As the horses raced, Fancy Pants came neck and neck with Serenity. They crossed the finish line requiring a photo finish. It was Fancy Pants that won. Serenity was in second place. George couldn't believe Landon's luck. He went to cash in the two tickets. When he came back, he gave Landon his winnings, one hundred dollars.

"Wow! I won."

"You are a lucky boy to have around," said George, "Here, have another beer."

Landon was getting used to the taste and took the alcoholic drink casually.

The evening proved to Landon that he was no boy. He didn't say that to George but he felt like a winner. He paid for every race and got carried away with his winnings. By the end of the evening he was hooked on the race track. He was very drunk by the time they left for the Lake. Mason stole money from Landon's winnings throughout the night. *What Landon didn't know wouldn't hurt him,* he thought.

"Gotta go, you comin' for poker tomorrow night, Mombo?" asked Mason.

"Yah, I'm bringing the gang with me. Bring Landon. He may bring me some luck."

"He'll be there."

George Mason drove the kid back home and practically carried him into his trailer. He tossed him onto the couch to sleep it off.

It was 1:00 a.m. when Victor looked out the window to see George's vehicle at the trailer. He surmised Landon was sleeping there. This ticked him off that he didn't have the decency to bring him home. He'd let it go this time but it was typical for Mason to be so inconsiderate. He went back to bed.

. . . .

The gang arrived with Mombo for poker at George's trailer. There was Nellie Westin, the thirty- year-old woman who dressed like a hooker with a black, leather mini skirt, a white top practically revealing her bosom and lace stockings with high-heeled ,shiny, knee-high boots, wearing dark, black make-up and piercings through her nose, ears and tongue with tattoos on practically every part of her body that was visible. Then there was Alicia Gonzalez, dressed in drab colours, gray and black capris, a navy top, no piercings but tattoos on her neck and hair, multi-coloured with orange, blue and pink stripes through her short hair style. Jude Roscoe was a man, thirtyish, who came wearing cut- off beige shorts, had a stubble face that hadn't been shaved for at least a week, brown hair, and carried a case of beer. George greeted his friends and introduced Landon as his lucky sidekick.

"I've asked Landon to sit in on our game tonight. He was my ace last night at the races and I have plans for him tonight."

"Let's see what kind of luck he brings you tonight, loser," said Jude. "You've been losing for the last three weeks."

"Are you going to get him prepared for the game with a little snort?" asked Jude. "It's only fair to initiate him."

"I'll get the stuff." George went to his room and came back with some white powder on a clear dish. The gang had mixed feelings about the initiation of the new kid. Jude rooted for Landon to inhale the stuff through his nose which he did. Landon immediately started to feel detached from his body and his mind was all fuzzy. Everything in his head became extremely over drugged. The voices were intensely loud. He didn't feel too good. He lay on the couch.

"Let's start the game." "He'll come around." "It's his first time." "You deal, George." Landon heard the voices but didn't know who was saying what.

The gang began their game. Landon was just the lucky charm George counted on as they all started with Black Jack while he lay on the couch. George won the first hand with over one hundred dollars. "I told you my luck would change with him."

They all knew George believed Landon had some magical gift over his fortune. Just when the gang was getting drunk and the air became cloudy with cigarette smoke, there was a knock at the door. George opened the door. "Is Landon here?" asked Victor.

"Yup." He pointed to Landon's body on the couch. "He's a winner. You can't take him home now. He brings me good luck."

"What have you done to my son, George?" asked Victor from the doorway with rising concern.

"Oh, he's had just a little initiation into the gang. He'll be fine. I'll send him home after our poker game."

Victor was angry. He said, "I'll take him home **now**," as he moved into the trailer and helped to lift Landon off of the couch, brought him to his feet and shuffled him out the door.

George hollered back at Victor, "He's my godsend. I'll see you tomorrow, buddy." George resumed his game and lost for the rest of the night.

CHAPTER 5

A crowd formed around the office with nosey campers, locals, and the team members from the second murder mystery event. The gathering watched the body being lifted into the EMS ambulance and the coroner got into the service vehicle. They were headed for the Queen Elizabeth Hospital in Charlottetown.

RCMP Staff Sergeant Rob Camden came over to see his kids. "Are you and your friends OK?"

"Yeah. What happened?" Trish asked.

"One of the workers here became a victim of crime. Your mystery club and the other people involved in the murder mystery weekend as well as campers and workers will be interviewed by Sergeant Frank Brown and Corporal Kurt Lewis. When they are done, I think you and your club should call it quits on the weekend and come home."

"Are you serious, Dad? Come home? Our mystery club has just viewed a dead body being taken from Ben's Lake. We have to follow our Camden Mystery Club proper procedures. We'll let you know when we will be leaving the Lake. Don't worry about us. We've got this."

"Charlie, use your own discretion and Trish, listen to your older brother."

"Right, Dad," said Charlie.

"Thanks, Dad," said Trish. "See you."

Fourteen-year-old Landon overheard parts of the conversation Trish and the Mountie were having.

"Is that your dad?" he asked.

"Yeah. Hey, weren't you the teen scaring the kids at the bonfire last night with the story of the Black Hoodie Man?"

"Yup. I do it all the time, whenever there is a new group of campers around," said Landon.

Trish had her photographic memory and her psychic awareness focussed on Landon. She noticed he was despondent over the death and appeared agitated. "Did you know George?"

"He said I was his lucky kid. When he took me to the horse races, I won and he won, too. Then he took me to his trailer to meet his gang of friends and said I was his lucky charm as he kept winning at poker whenever I was around. When I wasn't around, he kept losing. He introduced me to stuff about life that my parents would never show me."

"What kind of stuff?" asked Trish.

"Just stuff, I can't say. I might get in trouble."

"I won't tell. I'm a teenager too, you know. I know about booze and drugs and stuff like that," she persisted.

"Well, he gave me beer and other stuff like white powder you sniff. George had lots of it and he gave it to me every day for the past couple of weeks. Now that he's dead I won't have it any more and I need it."

Landon hung his head down and stared at his feet. "My dad would kill me if he knew I was sneaking out every day to get high."

"Do you think your dad knew when you were high or not?"

"I usually avoided him afterwards. I mean after I had a sniff I'd hang out at George's place or go to a wilderness campsite for a while. He only came and got me the first night when I had the stuff and carried me home. He was mad. He told me to stay away from George but I liked him and the way I felt once I had a sniff."

"Landon, you had an illegal drug dependency. The detectives will probably find the drug in George's trailer when they go and search his place. You won't be able to get the drug anymore."

"But I need it!"

"I can't help you but you are young and illegal drugs are bad for everyone."

Just then Trish noticed Sergeant Brown and Corporal Lewis come out of the office and begin to question some of the crowd around the headquarters. The two detectives were getting names and phone numbers from campers. Trish and her club made their way over to the familiar Mounties. "Would you like some help from our mystery club, Detectives?" asked Trish.

Cal was trying to keep the group of people social distanced from one another. Most noticed the signs on the ground and respected the COVID restrictions.

Brown saw the club inching towards them. "Hello, Trish and Charlie, I think we've got this. Maybe you could help Cal Morgan with the social distancing of campers."

"OK," said Charlie.

"We can organize the group as well," said Trish. She then proceeded to take the team members that did the murder mystery after the CMC last night and lined them up behind Victor and Lily. By this time some of the campers decided to leave, as they weren't interested in giving their names to the detectives. Trish, Charlie, Paul and the twins advised that they all stay, as everyone at the campground was a person of interest. Frank and Kurt announced that everyone remain in proximity of the office and have their names added to the list. The Camden Mystery Club helped to keep the crowd from departing.

Trish was pondering her conversation with Landon. She looked around but couldn't see him anywhere. Trish nudged Charlie. "I've got some news," she whispered. "I spoke to the guy who told the scary story at the bonfire last night and he is a person of interest. I don't see him right now but I have a hunch he could be a lead in this case."

"Really, Trish? You've got your premonitions already?"

"Yes, I do. His name is Landon and he's fourteen and has already experienced more than you or me or any of our club. He's been hanging around the trailer of George, the victim, and when Brown and Lewis get to investigate the victim's residence they will find evidence that he was dealing cocaine. I also found out that George has a group of friends that come over once a week for a friendly game of poker. Landon told me he was George's lucky charm and was hooked on sniffing cocaine. He looked agitated and fearful that he wouldn't get any more stuff to feed his habit. What do you think of that, Charlie?"

"Gee, Trish you've unraveled a lot in a short time. Maybe we should give Sergeant Brown and Corporal Lewis this information."

"Are you kidding? I told Landon I'd keep his information a secret. He confided in me. I can't expose him to the detectives.

I think he's gone off and hidden somewhere so that he won't be questioned by the RCMP."

The brother and sister Camden team contemplated their evidence. Meanwhile, the detectives finished up the compilation of names and phone numbers from the campers and workers at the Lake. Their obvious next step was to investigate Mason's residence. Cal told them which trailer was George's and led them to it.

When Kurt and Frank entered the trailer, they were overcome with the stench of rotten cigarettes and became aware of the mess of dirty dishes, ashtrays of cigarette butts, empty beer bottles and other alcoholic bottles, poker chips and cards, and bedding and clothes strewn about the room. "He wasn't a tidy person," said Lewis.

Wearing rubber gloves the two searched in miniscule detail the contents of the trailer. In the bottom drawer under the bed in the bedroom, Frank found a stash of white powder in a plastic bag. He tested it and said, "I've got something here. Looks like George dealt cocaine. Have a look, Kurt."

"Yeah, looks that way. Does he have a list of friends that he may be dealing with?"

"We'll have to keep looking."

Frank and Kurt checked every drawer and every piece of paper in the piles of shredded papers in the place. They found a beat-up, old telephone book and read a list of names scribbled on the inside cover, Mombo Katumba, Nellie Westin, Jude Roscoe, Alicia Gonzalez, and Landon MacEwen. "These may be leads in our investigation," said Frank. "MacEwen, wasn't that the last name of the couple we interviewed earlier? Victor and Lily? We didn't see a Landon. Maybe we should check it out. Hey, looks like we've found a stash of money." Frank Brown pulled out a sock from the dresser and started counting the pile as he pulled it out of the sock. "Holy cow, there's $10 000 here."

Kurt Lewis and Frank Brown took the money and telephone book and headed for the MacEwen house near the front of the campground, looking for Landon.

CHAPTER 6

Landon was in hiding. No one would find him in the depths of the forest where there weren't any campsites. He didn't know what time it was but looking up at the sky he thought it was around lunchtime. He had his cell phone with him. He sent a text to Mombo:

George is dead. Game off. Don't come. Tell gang.

He lay on the pine needles in the forest and pondered what his next move would be.

The detectives met up with Landon's father, Victor. "We'd like to see your boy, Landon. Is he around?" asked Frank.

"I don't know where he is. I haven't seen him since early this morning. What's this about? Is he in some kind of trouble?"

"No, we just want to interview him. We've met your other children but missed him. We've got to head back to the office but his name was found at George's place; so we'd like to check with him why he has been singled out by Mason."

Victor was disturbed. "I'll take the four-wheeler and have a look down the trail. I'm not sure why his name came up. He's a teenager and I don't always know where he is. He usually shows up at mealtimes."

"Thanks. That would be a big help."

Victor was tense and didn't want to find Landon but headed down the trail and into the woods on the four-wheeler.

Landon heard the four-wheeler from his hiding place. He lay still as the vehicle passed by him. Victor went to the end of the woods and turned around and headed back to the house.

"I looked everywhere for him," he said to the detectives when he returned. "I don't want to hold you up. You've got your work cut out for you, I imagine. I'll speak to him when he comes home and tell him you'd like to have a talk with him."

"Oh, by the way, do you know anything about a gang meeting at George's trailer for poker?" asked Brown.

"I don't know everything about George's friends but he usually has a game on Sunday nights, if that's any help."

"Thanks. That's a big help. We are heading back to headquarters. Please ask Landon to call. Here is my card," said Detective Brown.

"Well, it looks as if the detectives are leaving," said Trish as the RCMP car pulled out of Ben's Lake campground.

"Do we have anything to do here now that they've gone?" asked Josie Freeman, John's twin sister.

"I want to talk to Landon. I have a suspicion that there is more for us to find out here before we leave," said Trish to the mystery club members who were on the front lawn near the Lake. "I had a private conversation with him this morning and he lives in the house across from the office. He disappeared before the detectives could speak with him. I think we need to locate him, as he may have some information that could help in solving the murder for our mystery club."

The club members were in agreement to search for the teen. Cal came over to see them. "How's it going? You are welcome to stay at the Lake for the rest of the weekend but the murder mystery is over; so you can use the facilities at no extra charge."

"Thanks, Cal. We'll probably stay for a while. Now there is a real murder and this is what we do best, that is, solve crimes," said Trish.

"If there is anything you need from me, just let me know."

"Well, we were wondering how the victim was murdered?" asked Paul.

"George was stabbed with a knife."

"Can we see the crime scene?" asked John.

"I'm afraid the office is off limits for today, anyway. The detectives cordoned it off. They may come back later."

Paul was getting hungry. He suggested to the club that if they were going to hunt for the teen they had better do it on a full stomach. Josie, John and Charlie agreed. Trish had too much adrenalin to think of her stomach right now. However, she gave in to the consensus of the group; so they paddled back to their remote campsite and ate some of the food Paul had brought. As they were munching, sitting on sleeping bags on the ground, a faint voice could be heard coming through the woods. "Hello. Is Trish there?" said the voice.

"Over here. Yes, Trish is here. Landon, is that you?"

Landon scrambled through the brush and appeared at their remote campsite. "Have all the cops gone?"

"Yes, Landon, they are gone. Come here and have some lunch with us. You might be getting hungry," said Trish. "These are my friends, Paul, John, Josie, and Charlie, my brother."

Landon was hungry, as he had skipped breakfast and it was past lunchtime. He sat beside Trish and Paul served him a ham sandwich. He had scratches on his legs and arms from twigs and branches. He looked sheepish and wondered how much of his story Trish had told the others. When they started to include him in the story of the murder and told him how much they liked his scary story from the night before at the bonfire, he started to feel comfortable with them. He was cautious about his secret but no one pressured him into anything. Once lunch was over, Landon shared one of his many secrets with the group.

"So, you guys like to solve crime stories. You have much luck with that?" he asked. "I played poker on Sunday nights with George and some of his friends. There won't be any more games here at the Lake now that George is gone."

"I know," said Trish sympathetically. "But to answer your question we do have luck and skill in solving crimes. Right, guys?"

"Trish is right. We do solve mysteries," said Charlie.

"How will the friends find out there is no poker game tomorrow night?" asked Trish.

"I've already sent a text to Mombo to tell the gang not to come," said Landon as he pulled out his cell phone from his shorts pocket.

"That's good," said Trish; "do you know the names of the other friends?"

"Yeah. There is Jude, Alicia, and Nellie. I have their phone numbers right here on my phone." He showed it to Trish. Then he instantly put it away. He did not know that Trish had a photographic memory and was storing the names and numbers in her brain. She thought *I must remember this data.*

"You'd better keep those numbers safe," she said.

You never know who might want them.

"Hey, they are in my phone and it never leaves my body."

CHAPTER 7

Jessy Baird was a punctual person arriving at the Lake at 2:00 p.m. There was no evidence of a crime scene except for the office being roped off with yellow tape. Cal expected her and pulled her close for a big hug and a kiss. "Am I ever glad to see you; it's only early but I've been busy all morning and my phone has rung nonstop. I've been signing campers out because of the death. Most are afraid of getting involved and feel uneasy."

"I'm sorry you've been overworked. I was happy to hear the news. George is dead. Praise the Lord. Do you know who killed him? Do you have any suspects?"

"The detectives were here all morning. They have phone numbers and names of everyone who was staying at the campground. They searched George's trailer.

Whatever they found in there I don't know. They must have found something but they just collected things and left around noon."

"So you had to cancel the rest of the murder mystery groups? That's too bad. I know how much work you put into it. Did the teams leave?"

"One team left but there is still one team here. They are the Camden Mystery Club. They said they wanted to solve the crime and thought they'd stay around for a while. Imagine, they think they can solve the murder better than the police."

"You never know. It looks as if they are on their way over to see you now or at least one of the canoes is coming across the lake."

Trish and Josie decided to come over to see Cal and leave the boys to pack up the campsite. They waved to Cal.

"Hey, Cal," called Trish as they banked the canoe. We have a question. Do you have a record of names and phone numbers of who signed in on last Sunday evening? We need to take a look at your records."

"I keep the records for the COVID 19 restrictions and have the list in the office. Do you need it?"

"Yes, please."

Cal was the only one allowed to enter the crime scene as he went to retrieve the list. He came back with the information quickly. "What are you looking for?" he asked.

Trish skimmed the list and recorded the gamblers' names and numbers in her note pad. She knew Landon only had the first names in his phone but she needed their last names as well. "Just checking out who was here Sunday night. Thanks. Got what we were looking for. Club stuff. We are heading out soon. The boys are clearing the campsite. By the way, we found Landon or, I should say, he found us. He's OK. You can tell his parents."

CHAPTER 8

Sergeant Frank Brown and Corporal Kurt Lewis spoke with the coroner, Dr. Mack Pathius.

"Did you find any prints on the knife?" asked Lewis.

"Not one. The killer didn't leave a trace. I must tell you there was no struggle and death happened instantly. I'd say it happened between 11 p.m. and 12 a.m."

The detectives had one more person to visit at headquarters. They went to their boss, Staff Sergeant Rob Camden.

"We need three search warrants, Rob. Shall we head to the Court House?"

"What's your thinking on the matter?"

"We believe we have the names and cell phone numbers of George Mason's gang which we found when we were viewing the contents of his trailer. We also found a kilo of cocaine and $10 000 in cash hidden in a sock in his drawers. We've collected these for evidence. We need to interview these suspects and need the search warrants to obtain their addresses. One of the ways we can get their addresses is to contact the phone companies. There are three we know of here in Charlottetown, Telus, Rogers, and Eastlink. With your OK we'd like your go ahead."

"Well, it's Saturday and I believe the court house is closed until Monday. You may have to wait until Monday for your search warrants. A kilo of cocaine and $10 000? You've uncovered some very incriminating evidence. You have my permission to get the search warrants from a judge on Monday. I was hoping you'd come here to report. Now I'm heading home for what's left of the weekend and I think you should do the same."

"Thanks, Rob. We'll do the same," said Frank.

The twins, Josie and John, sent a text to their mom, Barb, to pick them up at Ben's Lake, while Trish, Charlie, and Paul piled into the old Toyota to head for home. The camping was over but the mystery club made arrangements to meet in the clubhouse in the basement of the Camden house at 7 p.m. Trish, Charlie, and Paul thought of different scenarios to get the addresses for the gambling gang that Landon had told them about. Trish's immediate reaction was to use the numbers to call them on the phone and ask them for their address but that didn't seem possible. How else could they get their addresses? Then Charlie thought that the detectives would likely get search warrants to view the gangs' applications for phone service.

"How many different providers are there in Charlottetown?" asked Trish.

Paul said, "There are Eastlink, Telus, and Rogers that I know of for sure. I bet that is how they will get the addresses needed."

"It's Saturday and the courthouse is closed until Monday. We are in a state of limbo until then," said Trish. "We can't get search warrants, but just maybe Dad will allow us to investigate by accompanying one of the detectives."

"Once we get home we can ask Dad," said Charlie.

"I have a lot of questions for the Club tonight. We'll see you tonight, Paul," as they dropped him off at his home.

"See you later," he said.

Cornwall wasn't far, as it was on the west side of Charlottetown where the Camdens lived. They noticed their dad's car in the driveway. *Good,* thought Trish.

"Do you have any news for us?" asked Trish as soon as she entered the bungalow and saw her dad reading the newspaper in the living room.

"How was your morning?" he asked.

"Fine, but we want to know what you've heard from Brown, Lewis and Dr. Mack Pathius."

Rob Camden knew his daughter, her hyper, anxious nature, wanting immediate results as soon as yesterday if that was at all possible. He smiled, "Yes, I've spoken to them."

"And?"

"Mack didn't find any finger prints on the knife. Frank and Kurt found cocaine and money in Mason's trailer. They are heading for the court house on Monday to get search warrants for addresses of some of George's friends. Are you happy now?"

"Can the Club get the addresses from you to help us with our investigation, please Dad?"

"We'll see."

"The Club is coming over tonight for a meeting if that's OK with you?"

"That's fine."

"Thanks, Dad."

The teens arrived for their meeting, kicked off sneakers and sandals at the front door and darted through the kitchen and down to the clubhouse which was in the basement. It was a hot, August day and Trish had cold, ice water in a pitcher to serve to the group. Paul as usual was late but he was excused as he came with some of the camping snacks left over from Ben's Lake.

Trish always opened the meetings. "Here is the news from above," as she pointed upward to the staircase where her father was. "There were no prints on the knife, there was cocaine and money found in Mason's trailer, and Brown and Lewis are heading for the court house on Monday to get search warrants for the gang that Landon talked about."

She let this information settle with the members of the club.

"How much money was found and how much cocaine?" asked Josie.

"I didn't ask."

"Did you ask for the addresses of the gang?" asked Paul.

"Yeah, Dad said we'll see. I don't know whether we'll get them or not and whether Dad will allow one of us to visit with the detectives when they make a visit to a home. But there is something needling me, a premonition perhaps, and I want to discuss it with you. It's Landon. Here, he is a fourteen-year-old teen living at the Lake befriending a fortyish, gambling, drug dealer and from what I hear lazy, no-good man. Landon spoke to me early this morning in private but I think what he said may help us with our criminal investigation; so I will share his news with you." All were silent as they allowed Trish to continue. "Landon went to the horse races with George two weeks ago and Mason placed his bets for him. The lucky kid won almost every race and George called him his lucky sidekick. Then George invited him to his trailer for the poker night with his 'friends'. Once again George won with Landon's presence. He gave him cocaine and Landon got high. Every time over the past two weeks George got Landon to snort cocaine and Landon was hooked. Now, here's the question? Wouldn't you think Landon's parents would notice something was wrong with his behavior? Wouldn't that give them some motive to kill George?"

"I think it would give them strong motive but Landon's parents live there. They work for Cal and why would they risk their lives, their home, their work to murder that creep, George Mason?" asked Charlie.

"What are his parents' names?" asked John who was drifting off while munching on a bag of chips.

"Victor and Lily MacEwen," said Trish.

"They would have a lot to lose if they planned a murder," said Paul.

"Don't forget a mother's love for her son is a very powerful motive."

"I agree."

"Nevertheless, I still think we should follow-up on the gamblers," said Trish. "I'm just giving you some food for thought. I'll see what I can get out of Dad in ways we can meet the gang. That's all for now. Time for the munchies. Thanks, Paul."

CHAPTER 9

Sergeant Brown and Corporal Lewis arrived in their supervisor's office at noon. "We have the addresses from search warrant information we retrieved this morning. We checked out the names and found out Nellie Westin and Alicia Gonzalez have their phone provider through Telus, Mombo Katumba uses Rogers, and Jude Roscoe is with Eastlink. We've typed up their addresses and it should be on your E-mail."

"That's great. You've been busy," Rob checked his computer and said, "Yes, it's here. Are you heading out this afternoon to follow up with them?"

"That's our plan," said Lewis. "Sounds good. Keep me in the loop." "Will do."

Once the detectives left the station, Rob thought of the Mystery Club and their request. He sent Trish and Charlie the E-mail he had just received and thought nothing more about it.

Trish and Charlie were together at home when the text came in. "We've got some work ahead of us. Brown and Lewis will be following up on these characters and we don't want to get caught in their path. I'll meet up with John and you can take Josie and we'll cut the job in half. Who do you want to meet first?" asked Trish.

"It doesn't matter. I'll text Josie and see if she can be ready to go on short notice. We need another car. Maybe Paul can get his parent's car and can drive you and John."

"Okay. Paul can get the car and John is ready to go," said Trish as she received two texts in the last few seconds.

"Josie is ready. I'm going to pick her up now. I think I'll go to Mombo's place first," said Charlie. "Then head over to Jude's. You can check out the women with John."

"OK. Paul will pick me up first; then we'll pick up John. You go ahead and we'll have a club meeting tonight to compare notes."

"See yah later."

"Tell Josie about the meeting tonight." "Right on."

Charlie drove the old Toyota out of the driveway. Trish ate a sandwich while she waited for Paul. He arrived within fifteen minutes. Trish had just finished her lunch. They picked up John and headed into Charlottetown to the address of Nellie Westin.

Paul waited in the car. They were outside a grey- blue apartment building, apartment number 307. Trish and John waited inside the secure building until someone came out and they walked in. They headed up the seedy-looking staircase with paint peeling off the walls to the third floor. This wasn't new for John and Trish, as they had made previous calls on possible persons of interest before. They were in front of the door of 307 and knocked. There was no answer. They knocked again. They heard shuffling towards the door. It opened a tiny crack.

"Hello," said the voice.

"Are you Nellie Westin?" Trish asked. The young woman appeared disoriented.

"Yeah, what do you want?"

Trish and John peered past the crack into the room. She was the only one there. "We know you play cards at Ben's Lake with George Mason. He died on Friday night. We've come to hear if you saw him the night he died. Were you at the Lake on Friday?"

"I need some stuff. You got any coke?" "You mean cocaine?"

"Yeah, I need it bad."

Nellie was in withdrawal. Her mascara was smeared and she wasn't going to open the door. She just stood there, helplessly needing a fix. Trish said, "We are part of a mystery club and we need you to remember if you were at Ben's Lake on Friday night. Were you there?" she repeated.

"I don't know."

"I will call 911 for you." Trish dialed the number and gave the address. John and Trish waited outside the door of the apartment until an ambulance arrived. Meanwhile Paul was wondering what was taking so long when he heard the emergency vehicle arrive at the entrance to the building.

Trish and John gave their names and Nellie's name and her condition to the EMS team.

"Well, we don't know whether or not she was at the Lake or not. She looked out-of-it. She needed help and you did the right thing to call 911," John said as they got back into the car and relayed what had happened to Paul.

"Are you ready to go to the next address?" asked the driver.

"Yes. We are going to see Alicia Gonzalez, Paul."

"She lives close to here. I checked her address out when you guys were at Nellie's. She lives in a townhouse around the corner."

"Hopefully she is home and we can get more information from her," said John.

Paul parked on the street a few townhouses away. Trish and John got out and walked to Alicia's place. Trish rang the doorbell. It was answered right away.

"Hello," said the woman. She was wearing navy shorts and a T-shirt. She appeared with a tattoo on her neck and had short spiked hair, multi-coloured, orange, blue and pink stripes.

"My name is Trish Camden and my friend, John Freeman and we are part of a mystery club. We were at Ben's Lake on the weekend and heard about George Mason's murder. We know that you knew him and we are wondering if you were at the Lake on Friday night?"

"I've already talked to two detectives this afternoon and told them I wasn't there on Friday. I usually spend time there playing poker on Sunday nights, which happened to be cancelled last night because of Mason's death."

"Do you remember the boy, Landon?" Trish asked.

"Yes, the poor boy was being used by George. He got the boy onto cocaine as well as my friend, Nellie, who also plays cards with us. I know Nellie must be having withdrawal symptoms by now. Have you seen her in your inquiries?"

"Yes, she is in bad shape. She's gone to Emergency in an ambulance."

"Oh, no, really?"

"Yeah. We called 911 and waited for the ambulance to arrive. Where were you on Friday night?" Alicia said, "I was home. I can't go out with all the COVID restrictions. Nellie was here with me. She was OK then but was anxious to get her fix on Sunday. Things didn't go the way we planned."

"Thank you very much for your openness in talking with us. We usually have doors slammed in our faces."

"That's OK. But one thing I must say, George Mason is a creep. And the poker gang would all wish him dead."

CHAPTER 10

The club met up at the clubhouse at 7 p.m. Paul was on time bringing left over munchies from the weekend. They got right down to business.

Charlie spoke first. "Josie and I met two very interesting characters today. First we saw Mombo Katumba. He looks to be 40ish and looks like a heavy- duty wrestler."

"With a half- shaved head, a colourful ponytail, a beard and lots of tattoos on his arms," Josie interjected.

"Yes, he's quite a character. We weren't invited in and once we told him why we were there he almost slammed the door in our face. If I hadn't mentioned Landon, he would have. But he had a heart for the kid and said Landon was mentored by George. I asked what he meant and he said the kid looked up to him and it was the first time a person ever looked up to him."

"I think George liked the fact he had Landon dependent on him. Mombo also gave the impression that George felt lucky to have Landon around. He won a lot of money at the horse races when Landon was with him. I think George used Landon," said Josie.

"I agree," said Trish.

Charlie went on; "the next person we met was Jude Roscoe. He was around 30ish with a slight build, about six feet tall. He had nothing kind to say about Mason. He said George ripped people off and used people to fill his pockets. Oh yeah, he didn't let us into his apartment either. Can you add anything, Josie?"

"Jude looked as if he hadn't shaved in a week, stubble face with brown hair. He was in a foul mood that we found his address. He also said George owed him money from last week's poker game. When we were standing at the door Charlie asked where he was on Friday night. Jude said he thought Mason got what was coming to him but he wasn't at the Lake on Friday. He was having a few drinks at a friend's house in Charlottetown."

"I think Josie would agree that Mombo and Jude both had animosity towards George. They hated him, yet they continued to play poker with him on Sunday nights; that's a real gambler's addiction. What did you and John find out?" Charlie asked his sister.

"Nellie is a crack addict needing a fix and she made no sense at all when we met her. I called 911 and an ambulance came and took her to Emergency. Alicia was quite helpful. By the way, she had already met with Brown and Lewis. She was concerned about Landon. She also said George Mason was a creep and all the poker players wished him dead. Alicia also said that she and Nellie were together on Friday night."

"So the detectives were already at Alicia's place and we didn't hear that they were anywhere else ahead of us," said Paul. "What's your premonition now, Trish?"

"I think we have to go back to Ben's Lake before Sergeant Brown and Corporal Lewis. I sense Victor MacEwen, Landon's father, has something to do with the murder."

CHAPTER 11

One week earlier

Victor and Lily were in the kitchen discussing their son, Landon. "I'm worried about him. Ever since he went to the horse races he's been spending a lot of time hanging around the office with George Mason. And have you noticed he's been absent-minded and in a daze all the time. I think he's on some kind of drugs," said Lily.

"What do you want me to do about it? I know Mason has drugged him. Last Sunday I had to practically carry him home from the trailer. I hate this and I feel helpless. It's hard to ground him from seeing him. After all, he's starting to make decisions on his own whether we like it or not."

"Well, something has to be done. You're the one to take charge. I can't get through to him and he's not a good influence on the rest of the family."

"I'll speak with Mason but I don't know what good that will do. Landon is so hostile when I mention leaving George alone and suggest doing a few chores around here."

"A few chores? He doesn't even pick up the clothes he takes off at night. Half the time he sleeps with the clothes he has on during the day. I can't even get him to load the dishwasher. He's in a fog and I don't trust him with his sisters or Broon."

"I know. I'll have a talk with Mason and see what's going on."

Victor left the house and found George sitting on the rocker at the front of the office. It was noon and already the stench of alcohol was evident on his breath. George was not a person you could have a normal conversation with. He was argumentative and negative and he didn't like to hear of anyone else's point-of-view. He also played by the book, the George Mason book of rules.

"Hi George, I'd like to talk with you about my son, Landon. He's been spending a lot of time in your company. You got him on any drugs or something? He doesn't appear to be himself."

"You accusing me of giving drugs to your boy? He likes me and is about the only person here at Ben's Lake who does. Nothing wrong with him. Leave me alone and don't harass me about trivial crap. I could sue you for defamation of character. Now get lost."

"This is not the end of our conversation. You won't see the end of me. I'm watching you. And another thing, leave my son alone or else."

"Whoopee, you don't scare me." George took another swig from his bottle and lit a cigarette. This was going to be a good day. *I just told Victor to take a hike*, he thought.

Victor was fuming when he entered the house. "That jerk, all we can do is try to protect Landon from Mason. Where is he, Lily?"

"He's dead to the world in his bedroom. It's almost one and he hasn't gotten up yet. I take it all didn't go well with George. What did he say?"

"I don't want to talk about it. We need a strategy and I can't think of one at this moment. I've got to cut grass today. Cal is depending on me."

"The girls took Broon out to play. When they get hungry, I'll make them sandwiches. I have to clean the washrooms for the campers, too. See you later."

CHAPTER 12

Tuesday following the murder

Jessy spent the weekend with Cal at the Lake after the murder. Tuesday morning the RCMP detectives came over to remove the yellow tape cordoning off the crime scene. They talked to Cal. "We are investigating all leads to this murder," said Brown. "Do you have any suspicions as to why George Mason was killed?"

"He wasn't real friends with anyone. He was a loner and a lazy thorn in my side. I don't even know why we became business partners, as he didn't pull his own weight around here. I think anyone knowing him would know that he was a no-good-son-of-a-gun. My girlfriend, Jessy, was actually happy to hear of his death. It makes my life a whole lot easier."

"Where were you the night of the murder?"

"I was at the campfire with the mystery teams and other campers. I always stay with them and put out the fire at 11 p.m. Then I went to my trailer and went to bed. I didn't kill George but I'm content that he's gone. A murder at the Lake isn't good for business. Why would I kill him to hurt my business during a COVID 19 year?"

"We have to ask the questions regardless. We have another couple of interest to interview. Is your handyman, Victor and his wife, Lily, around?"

"They live in that house." Cal pointed. "They work for me and have four children. They should be up by now," as he looked at his watch and saw that it was 9:15 a.m. Victor cuts the grass on the property and helps with maintenance. His wife cleans the washrooms and empties the garbage cans. They will only be too happy to help with your investigation."

The detectives said they'd keep in touch and went to knock on the MacEwen's door. It was Maggie who answered the door. "Are your mom and dad at home?" asked Frank politely.

"Who is it, Maggie?"

"Two policemen. They want to speak to Mom and Dad. Come here," she called.

Victor and Lily came out of the kitchen and shooed Maggie, her brother, Broon and sister, Greta outside.

"May we have a word with you?" asked Frank. "What is this about?" asked Lily.

"We are following up with interviews from Friday night's murder. Can we come in?"

"Put on your masks and you may come in," said Lily.

"My name is Sgt. Frank Brown and this is Corporal Kurt Lewis. We met you on Saturday morning. We've taken the yellow tape down, as we have the murder weapon. There were no fingerprints on the knife that killed George Mason. We didn't find anything in the office that would incriminate anyone, but we are here to ask you where you were Friday night."

Lily looked at Victor waiting for him to speak. "The whole family was at the bonfire until ten p.m.; then we brought the kids back home and once we got the kids to bed we called it a night."

"Neither of you left the house after returning from the campfire?" asked Lewis.

"That's right," said Victor.

"Cal Morgan said you have four children and I saw only three go outside. Who is your fourth child and where is he or she?"

"He is a teenager who sleeps in in the mornings.

Landon is still in bed," said Lily.

"We'd like to speak to him. Can you get him up?" "He's grumpy if he is awoken."

"We know all about teenagers. We'll make the rounds and come back in a while," said Frank.

The detectives busied themselves with visits with fishers and campers, and returned to the office for one more look around.

The Camden duo, Charlie and Trish, headed for Ben's Lake after stopping at Tim's for coffee. They weren't surprised to see the RCMP vehicle there, but Trish was getting antsy about the detectives getting a head start on finding the murderer. Trish saw them snooping around the office when they arrived; so they parked their old Toyota a ways down the dirt road and walked back to Landon's home. Trish knocked on the door.

"Good morning. My brother, Charlie and I, were here for the murder mystery weekend that ended up in a real murder and we'd like to talk to you," she said to Victor through her mask.

Lily came to the door to see who was there. "The police are hanging around to speak to our eldest son whenever he gets out of bed."

"Oh, you mean Landon. Yes I've met him and had a good talk with him on Saturday. He actually came by our campsite to meet our mystery club when we were packing up to head out. He appeared very upset about the death. He had quite a relationship with George Mason, if you know what I mean."

As usual, Trish did all of the talking while Charlie nodded. With masks on, the Camdens were standing in the doorway.

"What did Landon tell you about his relationship with George?" asked Lily. "What did you mean when you said, 'if you know what I mean'? We know a lot about our son and George."

"Well, you probably know that he was taking drugs supplied by George," Trish said as a matter of fact. "And he is experiencing withdrawal symptoms right now. That's why he's still sleeping at noon on a Tuesday morning. You have every right to worry about your son and you have motive to kill his dealer." Trish was over the top but knew she was going completely on premonition and speculation.

"Whoa. You are making quite the assumptions. I did not kill George nor did my wife. As far as we know, Landon has been showing signs of drug use but that is as far as your insinuations will go. We were at the campfire on Friday night and after Landon told the story about the Black Hoodie Man and Cal put the fire out, our whole family came back home and that was around ten o'clock."

"Well, the death occurred between 11 p.m. and midnight. You knew George didn't partake in the camp bonfires and you could have easily slipped out of the house and stabbed him," said Trish. "What I'd like to know is how did you know George was at the office at 11 p.m. on Friday night?"

"I'm not answering that question, as I'm not guilty," said Victor, "I think we've heard enough of your guesswork." Victor's eyes glanced towards Lily under the pressure of lying. Trish made a mental note of this.

"Come on, Trish. We've exhausted our welcome."

"Lily, I bet you know that Victor left the house late at night on Friday. Isn't that correct?" asked Trish as Charlie started to lead her down the walkway. "He probably asked you for a pair of gloves." Victor and Lily closed the door.

Charlie and Trish saw Brown and Lewis coming out of the office. It was obvious they had to speak. "Good morning, you two," said Sgt. Brown.

"Good morning to you as well," said Trish. "I see you've taken the yellow tape down. May we have a look?"

"Help yourself. We are done in there." "Have a good day, detectives."

"You as well."

Their cordial, respectful dialogue was reciprocated as each pair knew they were both after the same thing.

Charlie and Trish made their way to the office while Brown and Lewis approached the MacEwen house.

"Let's replay the scene on Friday night, Charlie," as they entered the office. "We've seen enough CSI crime shows to re-enact the event."

The two sleuths each took their parts describing how the murder took place. *Why was George at the office so late and not in his trailer,* thought Trish. They looked around, noticed the fridge and checked its contents -- worm bait, and a few beers. They saw the office receipt book and perused it, nothing out of the ordinary. Trish assessed the scene. George must have been busy doing something underhanded. He wouldn't be working overtime. The killer must have noticed the lights on in the office. Victor's house was so close to the office that he'd be able to see the lights from his living room window. Trish was sure Victor was the killer. There was no proof but Trish felt it, knew it, and she knew Lily was in on it as well.

CHAPTER 13

Staff Sergeant Rob Camden, Sgt. Frank Brown, Cpl. Kurt Lewis, and Dr. Mack Pathius were having a consultation in Rob's office when Trish and Charlie arrived at RCMP headquarters in Charlottetown.

"Hello, you two. We were just finishing up our meeting about the ongoing investigation at Ben's Lake," said their father. "Where have you been today?"

"We are just coming from there ourselves," said Charlie.

"It looks as if we've got a lot of suspects with motive but no evidence to prove anything," said Rob. "Do you have any news of significance?"

Trish wanted to say something alone to her dad but wasn't about to say anything incriminating in front of the other Mounties. Instead she said, "No but we'd like to hear about your meeting. Do you have any news of significance to share with us?" The detectives knew Trish and Charlie had a mystery club and knew they were at the Lake this morning while they were there. They were the police and were cautious about revealing their findings to the teenagers.

Alicia Gonzalez was a true friend to Nellie Westin. Nellie was sent to the Mount Herbert Detox Centre and Alicia wanted to visit her. Due to COVID 19 restrictions being somewhat reduced, Nellie was permitted to have one visitor. Alicia made a plan to see her on Tuesday afternoon. Nellie was in no shape for visitors, as she was experiencing cocaine withdrawal symptoms and was agitated and anxious. Alicia wanted to share her information about the two teenagers that had called 911 and had her sent to Emergency and from there to Mount Herbert. Nellie wasn't coherent about anything Alicia said. When Alicia left the Detox Centre she texted Jessy Baird. *Nellie is in rough shape. She's in detox for ten days. I'll take her to my place then. I need help to get her drug-free. She will need a recovery program.* Jessy knew this was not going to be an easy task. She had watched from afar the addiction that Nellie had. Jessy texted Alicia, *I'll help.*

Jessy was a nurse and was working for a doctor in Cornwall. When the pandemic occurred, her hours were cut; so she did some work at the Queen Elizabeth Hospital (QEH). Jessy was a good person with rose- coloured glasses, always seeing things in a positive light. That was until she got mixed up with women like Lily MacEwen and Alicia Gonzalez, both people whom she had met through her boyfriend, Cal Morgan, at Ben's Lake.

Cal and Jessy had been dating for a couple of years. Jessy was always doing thoughtful things for Cal. She knew he wanted a dog. As a surprise for Cal, Jessy had her name in at the Humane Society animal shelter hoping to get the perfect pet for Cal. On Wednesday she received a call from the shelter with the description of a black Labrador that was one year old and just the kind of dog Cal loved. She said she'd stop in after work which she did. The female was playful and affectionate. It had been spayed. Jessy took it on the spot, bought dogfood, a collar, a lead, and couldn't wait to give the love gift to Cal; so she headed for the Lake with the dog panting in the backseat of her Nissan. Cal was on the dock when Jessy arrived. He recognized her car and walked towards it. When she opened the backdoor of the car, the large animal jumped out. Cal couldn't get over the surprise. "What have we got here?"

"I wanted to get you a dog and I bought her at the Humane Society. It's yours."

"Wow. You've outdone yourself Jessy." The dog wagged her tail and nuzzled into Cal's legs. Cal was speechless. He never actually thought he'd have a dog. "Oh, Jessy, I love her. I'd like to call her Coal since she is so black. You've thought of everything. This is our baby until we have a real one someday. Why would anyone want to give her up?"

"The family that had her said they couldn't afford to keep her with their loss of tourism jobs during the pandemic. They also said she loves to swim and fetch sticks."

"You amaze me. You are so lovely. I love you." "I love you, too, Cal."

Coal became part of Ben's Lake and she loved to swim in the lake. Lily and Victor's children came over and took a real interest in the dog. Jessy had to leave to head back to town. She said she'd be out on the weekend. Before she left she mentioned to Cal she had heard from Alicia about Nellie and that she offered to help if needed.

CHAPTER 14

Earlier the day of the murder

Alicia was in love with Nellie. She was enraged at her addiction and George Mason was her drug dealer. She'd do anything to get her clean. And now George had Landon MacEwen on drugs as well. The poor kid, she thought. It was time that Alicia had a word with her sister, Lily. Alicia drove out to Ben's Lake in the morning.

She sat down at the kitchen table with Lily. "You know Nellie Westin and I are a couple and her drug use is affecting our relationship. You also know your son is high every day because of George. Victor doesn't have the guts to finish him off but you, my sister, have all the anger deep inside of you to take care of this menace. I'll pay you to get rid of him for good. Just think how normal our lives would be if we could get rid of George and the drugs. Landon and Nellie could live normal lives. For me, big sister, you've got the determination to terminate George Mason. I'll pay you $10 000 to finish him off. Think about it. The time has come to do something about this evil man."

Lily had similar thoughts. She knew Victor couldn't follow through. She and her sister had a tumultuous upbringing. Their father beat their mother and the two sisters would hide under the bed when fights occurred. She hated her dad. Their spineless mother put up with his abuse for too long. In their teenage years the two girls, fourteen and sixteen, ran away from the gambling, the drinking, and the abuse. They offered to take their mother with them but she wouldn't leave. Alicia and Lily left the house, hitchhiked out of Charlottetown and ended up in Halifax. They worked for two years as waitresses in a seedy part of the city and lived at the YMCA. When Lily was eighteen, she met Victor. He was so different from her dad. He didn't drink or gamble. He wanted to move to Prince Edward Island. At this time Lily heard her dad had died and her mother was alone. Lily and Victor were married, left Halifax with Alicia and went back to PEI. Alicia got a job waiting on tables in Charlottetown and Victor took a job in the city as a carpenter. Charlottetown became their home for fifteen years and Lily gave birth to their children. Victor heard about the handyman job at Ben's Lake and wanted to get out of the city. The family moved into the house at the Lake where they have lived ever since. Alicia continued to wait on tables and met her girlfriend, Nellie. They became a couple.

Lily could do this. It would take some planning. She knew she'd need gloves and a weapon. She took out her gardening gloves which she used to weed the vegetable garden in the backyard. She'd wait until the bonfire was out and the campers were asleep for the night. She knew George drank at the office on Friday nights. She'd tell Victor that she couldn't sleep and was going for a walk. He knew this wasn't her normal routine. She told him to stay in bed. She took a kitchen knife and her gloves and went to the office. George was standing by the counter when she opened the door. He looked surprised to see her. "Hello, George." Once he faced her, she didn't wait. She shoved the knife into the front of his body and he fell backwards. A splash of his blood hit her gloves. Lily felt no remorse. Lily left the knife protruding from his heart and headed out towards the garden. She found the hoe and dug a hole in between one of the drills and buried the gloves. Then she put the hoe back and went into the house. Victor was standing there in the living room. He looked at her. "Did you do it?" he asked.

"It's done. No more pain in this house. We'll get Landon help when things blow over."

Victor put his arm around his wife. "I'll stand by you no matter what."

"You're a far better person than I am. Tomorrow the manure hits the fan."

CHAPTER 15

Wednesday

Trish and the CMC met. Paul came with the last of the munchies from the mystery weekend. They were discussing the state of affairs at the Lake and Trish wanted to add her premonitions about the murder.

"Charlie and I met with Victor and Lily, Landon's parents. My gut feeling is that Victor murdered George. He could see the lights on at the office late at night from his living room window. He has motive. We have no evidence but I don't think any of the poker gang came out to the Lake late at night to kill George. It doesn't make sense that they would surmise that George would be in the office late on a Friday night. Victor had motive and access to the office after the bonfire. Another thing, I noticed him shift his eyes towards his wife when I accused him of the murder. He became defensive and said he didn't kill George."

"What we don't have is proof. We need some evidence, Trish," said Josie.

"I know. If only we had fingerprints or blood stains somewhere. Where do we go from here?"

"Well, we definitely won't be able to return to question the MacEwens again," said Charlie.

"Yeah, I kind of accused Victor of the murder and he became very unpleasant, I must say, me and my big mouth. What should we do as a club?"

"Maybe we have to look at things with new eyes," said John. "Let's go back to the Lake for a last swim before we head back to school. Cal will probably allow us a free swim in the Lake, wouldn't he?"

"That's fine with me. Does everyone want to go back to Ben's Lake for a swim? It's a hot day and a swim might be a good thing to do. Besides, we just might antagonize our killer if we go out there as a group. You never know what can transpire. Can you get your mom's car, Paul?"

"I've already got it for the day."

"OK. Here's the plan. Charlie and I will meet you three at 2:00 p.m. at Ben's Lake for a swim. Meeting adjourned. See you later."

Coal ran freely on the property and Trish and the Club were delighted to have the dog with them at the Lake. Cal signed them in and gave them permission to go for a swim. It was the least he could offer, since the weekend had ended so abruptly. Coal was eager to follow them and they enjoyed swimming with her, throwing sticks for her to fetch as they played in the water. Once they had their fill of swimming, they lay on the bank on their towels. Coal shook; then disappeared, bored with them. She was off looking for more adventure.

Cal was smoking some meat in the smoke shack when Coal came to his side wagging her tail looking for a treat. Cal had saved a bone for her. Coal savoured the bone and gnawed on it happily for a while; then took the bone in her mouth and headed for the loose earth in the vegetable garden. Here she found a spot where the soil was broken up; so she dug a hole to bury the bone. As she dug the hole she found something soft and tugged at it. Once she pulled it out, she continued to place the bone in the hole and covered it up with her snout. Proudly she carried the new- found exhibit in her mouth towards the bank where the mystery club members were resting.

"Coal, what have you got there? Let me see," said Trish. When Trish reached towards her, Coal thought it was a game and started to run away. Trish knew the dog was in a playful mood; so she just lay on her towel keeping an eye on the dog. Eventually Coal came over and dropped the new- found toy at Trish's side. Trish looked at what was in Coal's mouth and found it was a pair of cloth, gardening gloves. The pair of folded gloves had a stain on them, **a blood stain.** The gloves were covered in soil and dog saliva but there was a definite brownish-reddish stain on both gloves under the dirt. Trish's mind was a whirl. Was this evidence of the murder? What if the stain was from George Mason? Would it be possible to have a DNA test done on the gloves to see who wore them? This was definitely a possibility.

"Hey, you guys, Coal has found something very exciting. It looks as if he dug up a pair of gardening gloves with blood stains on them."

Charlie said, "the dog has saliva all over them and there is dirt on them but I also see the stains. Put them in a side pocket of your kitbag Trish and if we can make it to the RCMP office before it closes for the day they can probably send them off to Halifax for analysis."

"Let's go!" said Trish.

Charlie and Trish took the sample, picked up their towels and quickly dressed over their dried bathing suits. The other three said they would follow shortly but asked Trish to text them with any news.

In the car Trish said to Charlie, "this might be a breakthrough in our mystery. I noticed the gloves looked as if they were smallish, maybe for a woman. I thought Victor was the murderer but these gloves wouldn't fit on his hands."

"Don't get ahead of yourself, Trish. The evidence hasn't even been processed yet. Don't forget we have to send them off to

Halifax to get a DNA test done and that takes weeks to get a result."

"But can't they do the blood test here at the QEH lab?"

"Yes, I think you are right; but the DNA is what we want to know if we want a charge on a killer."

"We have to see Dad and he will get the detectives to send the evidence by courier. He will probably have the blood analysis and DNA done at the same time in Halifax."

They remained silent in thoughtful introspection for the rest of the trip into town. Charlie and Trish met their father in his office, explained the find and Rob called his detectives, Frank and Kurt, to come in to explain the new pair of gloves with possibilities. They were still in Trish's side pocket of her kitbag when Sgt. Brown removed them with rubber gloves. He thought to himself *leave it to the Camden teenagers to find a murder clue.* He packed up the gloves in a waterproof bag and the two detectives took them to the courier to be sent out by 5:00 p.m.

CHAPTER 16

Alicia Gonzalez picked up her partner, Nellie Westin, at the detox centre on the tenth day of her stay. Nellie was feeling more like her normal self and was happy to be going home.

"You can stay at my place for a while if you like. I've missed the old Nellie and it's good to have her back. The doctor said it would be a good idea for you to join a recovery program to support you during the next few months."

"A recovery program is not my bag. I haven't had any crack for ten days and I think I will stay with you for a while. I just need "us" to get better. I've been a total imbecile. I don't even know where to get the cocaine now that Mason is dead."

"Well, that's a good thing. I am happier to have you back to normal."

Alicia went to Mombo and Jude and mentioned to Nellie that she needed money to pay off Lily. They all pitched in for the worthy cause. Alicia took the accumulated money and paid Lily the $10,000 in cash in a brown envelope two weeks after

George's death. Lily wouldn't rat on her. Victor found the money in the envelope stashed in the bottom drawer of Lily's dresser. He knew better than to say anything about it to his wife.

Landon was off the drugs. He was starting to help out with minor chores like putting dirty clothes in the clothes hamper and making his bed. He still remained a typical teenager being bold, brazen, and rebellious with his parents and siblings. Victor and Lily treated him as if they were walking on eggshells. His temper erupted towards his sisters and his parents but they thought he was going through a lot of teenage emotions, developing his own identity and personality.

As the month of September arrived, the Lake wasn't as busy. Tourists in the Atlantic Bubble were heading back to school and work. Cal and Jessy spent weekends at the Lake. When Jessy wasn't nursing she offered to be of help to Nellie and Alicia. She also met up with Lily to share a cup of tea and to ask about Landon. The Camden Mystery Club members were back in school waiting for the DNA results from Halifax.

The results came in to the RCMP Headquarters and Dr. Mack Pathius informed his supervisor, Staff Sergeant Rob Camden. "The blood stains were a match with the blood sample sent with the gloves. It belonged to George Mason. A DNA match to a comparison of a sample on file was detected in the interior of the gloves. You'll never believe it -- the DNA match was made through Ancestry.com to a Lily Gonzalez, of Spanish origin. There was also DNA from a Labrador Retriever dog as well as DNA from an unknown source."

"Ancestry.com? That's a surprise. Well, that's a stroke of luck. Lily Gonzalez MacEwen has a DNA sample with Ancestry.com. I'll send Frank and Kurt to pick her up. Thanks for the report, Mack."

"If only all cases were this easy."

Rob repeated the news of the report to his detectives and they chuckled over the Ancestry.com match. "DNA proof every time," said Kurt.

"It's scary to think one's DNA can be traced through that method. We'll head out to Ben's Lake and make the arrest."

"Try to make it as humanely as possible and take a search warrant. You may need to check out the house for any other clues."

"We will."

The two detectives picked up a search warrant from the courthouse and headed for Ben's Lake. It was noon when they arrived. The kids were in school which made it easier to be less intrusive. With masks on, the detectives knocked on the door and Victor answered it.

"We have a search warrant and are here to arrest your wife, Lily, for the murder of George Mason."

Lily was in the kitchen preparing a sandwich for lunch when Victor answered the door. She sat at the table eating her ham sandwich and had a foreboding feeling that things were going to drastically change in her life.

Frank and Kurt came into the kitchen, handcuffed Lily and informed her of her rights. They let her sit there with her husband while the Mounties searched the house. They found the brown envelope in her dresser drawer with the money Alicia had given to her. They took this as evidence.

Victor had his arm around his wife while the search continued. Lily asked Victor to pack a bag for her which he did. Once the search was over and Victor passed the suitcase to Frank, the detectives put Lily in the backseat of the police car.

"Victor. Tell the kids I love them," were her last words spoken as the vehicle left for the police headquarters.

Rob Camden arrived home for supper. Trish had prepared spaghetti. Charlie was home as well. It wasn't usual for the three of them to sit down together for a meal. Rob said, "We have Lily Gonzalez MacEwen in custody for the murder at Ben's Lake. The DNA on the gloves you found was identical to hers and the blood sample matched George Mason's. Frank and Kurt picked her up today."

"I'm surprised. I thought it was Victor that killed George. I had a premonition about him. I thought Lily may have helped him but I was sure that Victor murdered George. Wait a minute, you said Lily Gonzalez MacEwen; that name is familiar. Gonzalez is the last name of Alicia Gonzalez. They must be related."

"It seems Alicia Gonzalez is Lily's younger sister. Well, DNA tests don't lie. It was good you brought the gloves into the station. The case is conclusive."

"Oh, yeah, I remember the gloves appeared to be too small for a man's hands; so it was Lily."

"Mombo, Jude, Nellie and Alicia were all gamblers with George. Weren't they incriminated in the case at all? Did the detectives find anything in their search of the house?"

"They found a large sum of money in a large, brown envelope. The crime lab is checking the envelope for fingerprints. Sgt. Brown has interrogated Lily in an interview room about the murder and the money. She admitted to the murder but refused to say how she came up with the $10, 000. My supposition is that she was paid by someone for the murder. This would lead us to a case of someone aiding and abetting the murder."

CHAPTER 17

Trish texted the Club members the news of the day and went to bed that night thinking about all she had heard. Who would pay for the murder of Mason? Why was Lily protecting the identity of the person who gave her the money? Could it be the fact that blood was thicker than water and she was protecting Alicia, her sister? If so, where would Alicia get that kind of money? Did the circumstances have anything to do with the gang members after all?

Trish fell into a tumultuous night of dreams. The next morning she awoke feeling groggy. She knew she had to pay a visit to Alicia Gonzalez and texted John to see if he'd go with her. He said he would and Charlie didn't need the car; so they were able to leave Cornwall after breakfast.

Trish picked him up. "What's on your mind, Trish?" "I think the money found in Lily's dresser is linked to her sister. What I can't figure out is how did Alicia come up with that kind of money?"

"Maybe she borrowed it from someone else."

"That's what I've been thinking. Who would she turn to in that case?"

"Maybe another gang member?"

"Well, there are only four gang members, Nellie Westin, Mombo Katumba, Jude Roscoe, and Alicia Gonzalez. Anyway, I want to question her about the money and I need you to come with me to her house."

They knocked on the door of Alicia's house. Nellie answered the door. She looked a lot better than the last time they saw her. "Hello, Nellie," said Trish, "Is Alicia home?"

"Alicia. You are wanted at the door."

Alicia came to the front door and remembered speaking to the teenagers once before.

"Hello, you two, what do you want?"

"Your sister, Lily, was taken to police headquarters yesterday. They spent time interrogating her about George Mason's death. They have a DNA match that proves she killed him. The detectives also found a brown envelope with a large sum of money in it at Lily's house."

"I didn't know. How is she? Is she still at the police station?"

"I'm not sure at this point. They've probably taken her to Sleepy Hollow jail."

"I must go and see her."

"Do you have any idea how the money, $10 000 was found in a brown envelope in her dresser drawer? Where did it come from?"

"I don't know," said Alicia looking sad at the news about her sister.

Trish sent a text to her father to check the whereabouts of Lily MacEwen. He sent a text to say she was taken to Sleepy Hollow.

"I have it confirmed that Lily is at Sleepy Hollow jail."

"I will see her today," said Alicia. "Good-bye," as she shut the door.

Trish and John left but as they were leaving Trish said, "I think she knows something about the money but she didn't say anything."

"The crime lab may be able to detect fingerprints on the brown envelope," said John.

"I'm going to drive over to the RCMP office. Are you OK with that?"

"Sure. You are the driver."

Trish pulled into the Mountie headquarters and she and John hopped out of the old car and went inside. Trish led the way to her dad's office. "Any news on the case, Dad?"

"Hello, John. The girls in the lab are checking for fingerprints on the brown envelope. I haven't heard anything yet. I'll let you know if I get an update. You know things don't happen instantaneously, Trish. Now I'm very busy; so I should know more before the end of the day and I'll let you know when I get home for supper. See you later."

"OK, Dad. See you tonight. Have a good day."

CHAPTER 18

Charlie was at a meeting when Rob got home to greet Trish who took over the job of cook in the kitchen for her father when he was late. She wanted to pounce on him for information but noticed how tired he looked. All she said was, "Supper's ready."

"Thanks, Trish. I'm starved. Something smells good. Did you make Shake N' Bake chicken?"

"Yes and baked potatoes with broccoli."

"It's been quite a day," he said as he served up his plate. Trish served her own and they sat at the table. Trish was just itching to get any news.

Once Rob started to eat he began to feel revived. "I bet you're antsy about my news, aren't you?"

"You know me, Dad. Do you have anything significant to share?"

"Well, there were quite a few fingerprints on the brown envelope. Of course, Lily's prints were there but there were prints of four other people's fingerprints as well. Some were just partial prints but when the girls started checking the money that came in the envelope they found the same prints on some of the money. It looks as if four people pooled their money in the brown envelope."

"Did you find any of the names that correspond with the fingerprints?" asked Trish.

"Well, yes. What's your guess, Trish?"

"Alicia Gonzalez, Nellie Westin, Mombo Katumba, and Jude Roscoe. Am I right?"

"I don't know how you do it, Trish, but you are absolutely right. How did you know?"

"They are the gang members who played poker with George Mason and Alicia said to me once that the gang would all wish he were dead. They helped pay for his death."

"Well, I sent you a copy of their addresses and Frank and Kurt are rounding them up and bringing them in for aiding and abetting the murder of George Mason. It looks as if your club can have a party tonight."

"I'll text them and we'll be down in our clubhouse. Oh, just one more question. What does the RCMP do with the money they found in George's trailer?"

"Once it goes through the courts, any money confiscated is used for education, training and equipment for the RCMP needs."

"And one more thing, will the money the gang paid for the murder get used for the same thing?"

"Yes, my detective daughter. You kids had your wits about you to help solve this case."

"Thanks, Dad."

BOOK 5:

MILL RIVER MALICE

CHAPTER 1

The Quinn family lived up the road from Mill River Resort in Prince County, Prince Edward Island. There were Violet and David Quinn with their three children, Mary and Bridget, their biological daughters, and Brett their adopted son. The family lived an extremely religious life and because of this the parents felt the children were protected from the evils of the world. Violet home schooled her three children until they were teenagers and then they went to high school. Mary, the eldest, became best friends with a classmate named Jennifer. They were inseparable and spent time visiting each other's homes. Jennifer's home life was much more open and Mary began to watch television for the first time, as it wasn't permitted at her home. Jennifer was attracted to her friend physically; so one day when she was visiting Mary's home and they were in Mary's bedroom, she kissed Mary on the lips. Mary felt something wonderful, but also embarrassment, fear, shame, and guilt. She knew her parents wouldn't approve of this sign of affection but Mary and Jennifer were best friends, the first and only friend that Mary ever had; so Mary began to allow Jennifer to touch her in intimate ways when they were alone.

After high school graduation, Mary got a job at Mill River Resort as a housekeeper. Jennifer left Prince County and went to UPEI in Charlottetown to study sociology and education. Mary and Jennifer wanted to correspond; so Mary rented a post office box in Alberton. She was permitted to take her driver's licence and eventually was allowed to take the car to work. From there she would drive the short distance to the Alberton post office to mail and receive correspondence from Jennifer. Cell phones were not allowed in her home and although her parents bought a computer for the teenager's schoolwork, Mary no longer could use it, as she was a working girl now. Eventually Mary felt stifled at home and at the age of twenty she moved into Sean and Martha Gallant's Alberton rooming house which had a TV in the living room.

Mary Quinn worked diligently at Mill River Resort and her effort, friendliness, and eagerness to learn the business of the resort quickly resulted in her receiving promotions and at the age of 28 she became the assistant manager. Jennifer no longer kept in touch with Mary but Mary met a young man, Benny Dorset, who worked as the head chef at Mill River and they began dating. Mary had friends through the workers at the resort, Rodney Huff, a black, Jamaican bookkeeper, Omar Singh and Cash Hussain, cooks in the kitchen, and Jack Rogers, who looked after recreational activities on the grounds. Mill River Resort had many other part- time employees looking after maintaining the property and keeping the high standards of exceptional comfort at the resort.

On one particular day Mary received a letter in the mail from a lawyer in Charlottetown saying she was to inherit $20 000 from the estate of her late Aunt Hilda, an aunt on her father's side of the family and one she never met. The cheque would be sent shortly. Mary was surprised and delighted with the news of her inheritance. Mary's life at age 28 was just about perfect until one day everything in her happy life came to a halt.

On this certain day a short time after she received the inheritance she opened her mailbox and found a note, "I know about you and Jennifer. You must pay $1000 or I will share your secret love affair." Mary was trembling. Who knew about her and Jennifer so long ago? The note said for her to transfer the money from her bank account to an anonymous bank account by December 5, 2020, which happened to be tomorrow's date. She was terrified that someone would share her very dark secret; so she made the transfer and hoped all would be back to normal which wasn't the case. Three days later she received another message from the anonymous blackmailer to transfer $5000 into the account by December 12, 2020. Her inheritance was quickly becoming depleted, but she was so full of fear, shame, and guilt that she paid one more time in the hope that this problem would be resolved.

Staff Sergeant Rob Camden and good friend, retired Mountie Coady Freeman, were having breakfast on the Saturday morning before Christmas at Sam's Restaurant in Cornwall. They were chatting about how their teenagers were growing up and wanting to plan a getaway weekend for their families. They had heard good things about Mill River Resort and had picked up pamphlets about the resort at the entrance to Sam's. They agreed to plan a long weekend to break up the doldrums of the winter. They decided on giving the kids a Christmas surprise to be used in January. "I know

Trish will like the cross country ski trails, salt water swimming pool, and outdoor skating rink. Charlie may or may not join us, as he is having thoughts of spending time with his new girlfriend."

"I still think Josie and John will both like the activities available at the resort. Barb likes the pool and sauna. We can wrap up these Mill River Resort brochures as their gift."

"It will certainly help to have something to look forward to and you and I can relax in one of our housekeeping suites, that is, if you are in the mood to unwind."

"You've forgotten I'm already unwinding ever since I retired last year. It's you that needs to put your feet up."

"Yes, indeed. COVID- 19 has its challenges. I'm hoping next year will be easier for all of us. Well, it is always good to catch up with you, Coady. I must go and finish my Christmas shopping. See you on Christmas Eve at your place."

Trish and Charlie Camden lived with their dad in Cornwall. Their mom had died in a car accident when they were small, and Rob had his mother look after the children when they were young. Nana resumed her independent life when they became teenagers; so presently the three of them lived alone. The Camden Mystery Club was an integral part of Trish's life and the basement of the Camden home was the clubhouse for the group. The club consisted of Trish and Charlie, twins, Josie and John Freeman, and Paul.

Trish was excited with the gift from her dad on Christmas morning that her family and the Freemans were going to Mill River Resort for a three-day weekend in January. She had never been there. She read the brochure. "Cross country ski trails, tubing hill, outdoor skating rink, sleigh rides, a salt water swimming pool with a 90-foot water slide, a whirlpool and sauna. Wow, Dad, this looks great! They even have a dining room with their famous Burger Love called, 'The Thrill in the Mill'. I'm going to try that. This is awesome."

"What about you, Charlie? Are you game to come along?" asked his dad.

"Yeah, it sounds cool."

Once they had opened their gifts, Trish stuffed the turkey and put it in the oven. After a Christmas brunch of eggs, bacon and toast, she received a text from John about the special weekend plans for the two families in January. John and Josie were as excited as Trish. The Christmas day was a very happy one for them all.

The weekend reservations were made and the Camdens and Freemans arrived in mid- January at Mill River Resort. They were met at the front desk by Mary Quinn, the assistant manager which Trish noted on her name tag. "Welcome to Mill River. Your rooms are ready and your hotel attendant will show you to your suites." Trish's sixth sense was tingling. She saw something in the assistant manager's eyes that showed nervousness.

"Do you have all the activities listed in your brochure for us to attend?" Trish asked.

"Yes. We have a recreational director, Jack Rogers, who is available to guide you into whatever events you wish. He has an office down the hall. I would suggest you follow the bellman and drop off your luggage first," said Mary.

"My name is Trish Camden. Have you worked here for a long time, Mary?"

Mary didn't want to engage in personal conversation. She did her professional part by explaining the resort's published details. She was unable to answer Trish's question with anything more than a weak, "not long." Trish let her attempt to converse with Mary go and followed her dad, Charlie and the bellman to their suite which was across the hall from John and Josie's room.

"This is awesome!" said Trish. "I'm going to go for a snoop around, Dad. I'll see you later."

CHAPTER 2

ary Quinn kept in contact with her parents. She'd send them Christmas cards in the mail, visit once a month, and call them from time to time. She never mentioned the blackmailer to them. Throughout the Christmas holidays she worked. The next anonymous note came on December 29, 2020. This time the crook demanded $8000 by January 1, 2021. She worried and fretted about meeting the pressure of the blackmailer's ultimatum. Her new boyfriend, Benny, knew something was wrong. He asked her why she was so agitated. She couldn't tell him. She couldn't tell anyone. She had the inheritance money and therefore made the payment on January 1. Mary settled into her work. She pushed all her fears and anxieties down into the pit of her stomach and took on the appearance that all was well in her life.

Benny prepared special meals for Mary when they were alone at his apartment. He had been to the Culinary Institute in Charlottetown for his training. He was kind and fun to be with. She told him about her childhood and being raised in such a strict home. She never mentioned Jennifer.

Bridget, Mary's sister, left home and moved to Charlottetown and got a job as a school secretary. Brett, her brother, spent time searching on the computer for information about his biological parents. He worked on a mussel boat and continued to live with his adoptive parents.

Mary couldn't afford a car. She got rides to work with a few different people who worked at the resort and lived in Alberton. It was the middle of January when the next demand for money came. This time the ultimatum was outrageous; $10 000 by January 15, 2021 or else I tell all. It was January 15 today and Mary had not yet met the blackmailer's demand. It was the same day that she met the guests from Cornwall, the Camdens and the Freemans. She knew she was unable to give the greetings to the crew when they arrived at the resort. The girl asked her a question about how long she had been working at the resort and all she could come up with was 'not long'. She had been there for eight years; yet she was so worried she just wanted the guests to disappear from her sight. Go to your rooms. Check out the amenities, she thought. Leave me alone.

Mary put in her allotted time for her shift. She got off work at 6 p.m. Before she left, she mentioned to Rodney Huff, the bookkeeper, that she didn't have a ride home. He said he was unable to leave the front desk and just when she was getting her coat and boots a call came to the front desk which Rodney answered. It was from a cell phone asking if Mary Quinn had a ride home that night. He said no. Mary was ready to leave and thought of hitchhiking a ride to Alberton. It was a dark night when she stepped outside in the lights of the resort. She walked down the driveway towards the highway. Just then a person taller than herself wearing a black face mask approached her. The voice said, "Where's my money, Mary? It was due in my bank account today and it's not there."

Mary was terrified. It was a man's voice and there was something familiar about it.

He grabbed her by the throat. She gasped for air. He pulled her onto the beginning of a ski trail. She struggled, grasped at his neck, felt something fall, and tried to escape but he was much stronger than her.

With his gloved hands he choked her until she no longer moved. Mary was dead. The killer dragged her down the ski trail into the woods. He shuffled snow on top of her body. Then he left her there in the cold still of the night.

CHAPTER 3

Trish explored the resort indoors and made plans to go for a swim with John and Josie after dinner.

It was getting dark outside so she decided to stop to see the recreation director to ask for a guide to the outdoor activities. Jack Rogers was in his office. Trish quickly introduced herself and asked about cross country skiing and a map of ski trails on the property. She also wanted to know about the skating rink and tubing hill. Jack was a young, athletic, attractive man of about 30. He explained all of the amenities in detail to Trish, gave her a map of the ski trails, and said the weather looked fine for the next day with temperatures around -1 degree Celsius. Trish thanked him. She was getting hungry and looked at her watch. It was after 6 p.m. and so she went to the suite to see if Dad and Charlie and the Freemans were ready for dinner in the restaurant. She found them all waiting for her return so that they could head to the restaurant. Trish ordered the Burger Love hamburger and so did the Freeman twins. They had a family dinner together like old times.

"I'm so full I think we'll have to wait an hour before we go to the pool," said Josie at the dinner table.

"I agree," said Trish. "Are you going to come for a swim or to the sauna tonight, Barb?"

"I'm going to leave the pool to you young folks tonight. I'll check it out tomorrow."

"Have you any plans for tomorrow, Trish?" asked her dad.

"It's supposed to be sunny and fairly mild. I'd like to try the ski trails in the morning. Does anyone else want to cross country ski in the morning?"

"You know I'll go," said John. "Me too," said Josie.

"I'd like to go as well," said Charlie.

"Great. The Camden Mystery Club will hit the trails, all of us except for Paul," said Trish.

After dinner the teens were keen to try the water slide in the pool. They swam and tried the whirlpool and sauna. Charlie was the first one to leave. He headed back to the room followed by the others shortly afterwards. It was 10:00 p.m. when they settled down to watch a television show. Rob retired to his room. Trish and Charlie watched a crime show before lights out at 11:00 p.m.

The Camdens and Freemans had breakfast in their suites with food that they brought from home. It looked like a perfect day. The sun was sparkling on the light, fluffy snow. The teenagers in their winter apparel left the main building, put their skis on and headed for the closest ski trail. As always, Trish was in the lead, skiing at a swift pace when all of a sudden she saw a mound of snow concealing what seemed to be a body.

"Hey you guys, look here." She took off her skis and pushed the snow away from the victim. The others followed her gaze and removed their skis as well.

"She was at the front desk when we arrived yesterday," said Charlie.

"Her name is Mary Quinn. I saw her name pinned on her uniform yesterday. She must have been here all night," said Trish. "We've got to report this to the local police."

Immediately Trish took her cell phone from her ski jacket pocket to phone 911. Instinctively she approached the body and felt Mary's jacket pocket. She retrieved Mary's cell phone and hid it in her own pocket. Then she made the call. She explained the location and the four of them waited for the RCMP to arrive. They didn't have long to wait. Within fifteen minutes two Mounties appeared at the scene, Constable Evelyn Clement and Corporal Harry Paine from the West Prince RCMP station. Charlie sent a text to their dad, Staff Sergeant Rob Camden, head of the RCMP for the whole island. The constable and corporal viewed the body. Constable Evelyn Clement knew the victim. "Mary Quinn is her name," she said to her corporal. "She's from around here. I know her sister, Bridget, and brother, Brett. She came from a strong, religious family."

Once the Emergency Medical Service vehicle arrived, Rob Camden was by the side of the teenagers. He sent word to Dr. Mack Pathius, the coroner, to meet him at the Prince County Hospital to determine the time and cause of death. He said to the club members, "You stay here and try to enjoy yourselves. First I'll text Coady to let him know the news. Then I'll meet up with Mack at the hospital in Summerside and the Mounties here will start the protocol of visiting the family and interviewing people around Mill River."

"Dad, we can look into Mary's work place as well," said Trish.

"Just don't get in the way, Trish." "We won't."

Trish didn't want to leave Paul out of the club investigations; so she texted him to see if it was at all possible for him to find a drive or borrow his parents car to come up to Mill River. She didn't get a quick response. The four of them decided to put their skis away and meet in the Camden suite to plan a series of people to interview. They knew the detectives would go to the Quinn family first to break the news which left them to roam the resort and break the news to some of Mary's fellow workers.

"The manager should be notified first," said Charlie. "Can one of you check Mill River Resort on your phone and find out the name of the manager here?"

"I have it. It's Garth Spencer," said Trish.

"Good. Do you and John want to speak with him?

Be compassionate and share your condolences. I think Josie and I should wait until you've made the first contact before we go any further with our interviews. Mr. Spencer may want to hold a meeting to inform the staff of her death."

"Sure. John and I can handle this. Let's head to the main office and see if Mr. Spencer is there."

John and Trish met Garth Spencer in the office where he was sipping on his morning coffee. Trish explained to Mr. Spencer how she and her fellow skiers were on the trail and happened upon the body of Mary Quinn. She offered their condolences in a very kind way. Garth looked surprised.

"I've been catching up on paper work here. You say an EMS vehicle was here to pick up the body? Why am I just getting informed now from a couple of teenage guests? Why didn't an RCMP officer have the decency to come into the resort and tell me in person? I'm in shock. Poor, Mary. She was one of the best. How did she die?"

"The body was taken to the Prince County Hospital where the coroner will determine the cause of death. Dr. Mack Pathius will be in Summerside this morning. My dad is Staff Sergeant Rob Camden and he and his retired Mountie friend, Coady Freeman, also guests here at the resort, are going to meet him there. The two Mounties that arrived at the scene are going to the Quinn residence to share the news. They probably didn't think of coming into the office; that is why John and I are explaining the news to you now."

"I must inform the staff of this tragedy. Thank you for your time. I must make several calls and collect the staff in the front foyer."

"May we come to hear your announcement?" asked Trish.

"Certainly. I may need your assistance. Did you say you were skiing on a trail with others?"

"Yes, my brother and John's sister were with us.

Shall we ask them to attend the meeting as well?"

"Yes. Now excuse me. The meeting will be brief and will commence at 10 a.m."

Trish and John headed back to the suite to inform Charlie and Josie of their encounter and tell them that they were to meet in the front foyer with the rest of the staff at 10 a.m.

CHAPTER 4

Constable Clement and Corporal Paine pulled into the driveway of the Quinn farm home. "This isn't going to be easy," said Paine to Clement.

"Telling the sad news of a death to a family member is a first for me."

"Well I'm here to support you. We will do it together."

The two Mounties rang the doorbell. The door was answered by a woman in her early fifties. She wore a dress in a plain burgundy colour, her hair was tied back into a bun with wisps of gray appearing through her brown wavy curls. She seemed surprised to see RCMP officers at her door.

"Hello. Can I help you?"

"Is your husband at home?" asked Paine.

"He's in the barn. Shall I go and fetch him? Why have you come? Is there something wrong?"

"Please get your husband. We'd like to speak to both of you."

The woman was startled with the request. She left the two officers at her doorway and headed out back towards the barn. When she returned she had her husband with her.

"May we come in?" asked Clement.

"Please come in and have a seat," said the man. "My name is David and my wife's name is Violet. Can you tell us what this is about?"

"We have come to inform you that your daughter, Mary was murdered last night. We are very sorry for your loss."

"Oh, no," cried Violet grief-stricken with the news. "How could this terrible thing have happened?" David Quinn put his arms around his wife to hold her sorrowful body and keep himself from collapsing.

"We found her body on a ski trail at the resort this morning. She was there since last night. Do you have any idea who could do such a terrible thing?" asked Clement.

The couple was in shock. They looked at each other with tears in their eyes. "We don't know who would do such a thing," said David.

"Do you know where she lived? Her friends? Any enemies? Her coworkers?" asked Paine.

"We know she lived in a boarding home in Alberton. I believe it was Sean and Martha Gallant's home. I have a birthday card in its original envelope with a return address on it. I can get it for you," said Violet through her heart-felt tears as she got up from the sofa and went to her bedroom to retrieve it.

"Thank you. That would be very helpful. Does she have any siblings?"

"Yes. Mary has a sister, Bridget, who lives in Charlottetown and a brother, Brett, who still lives at home but he's at work today. We'll have to tell them the news," said David.

"Yes, they should be informed. We are very sorry to have to break this news to you. Do you have a support network of friends to help you through this tragedy?" said Paine.

"We have our church family," said David.

Violet returned with the envelope and passed it to the detectives, then returned to her husband's arms.

"Please call your church. It's not good to be alone with this news. Thank you for the envelope. We'll be on our way." The Mounties got up and made their way to the door.

Once they were back in the police car Evelyn Clement said, "That was tough. I feel so bad for them."

"Yeah, telling the parents of death to one of their children no matter the age is a tough call. I think we should head to Alberton and see the Gallants."

"You're the driver. Let's go."

The RCMP detectives remained silent as they drove the short distance to Alberton. They found the boarding house and knocked on the door. Sean answered it. "Good morning, officers. What brings you here so early in the morning?"

"My name is Corporal Harry Paine and my partner here is Constable Evelyn Clement, may we come in."

"Certainly. What's this about?"

"You run a boarding house and one of your guests is Mary Quinn. Is that right?"

"Yes. She is a lovely young woman. She works at the Mill River Resort. She didn't come home last night which is unusual for her but we thought she may have spent the night with her new boyfriend, so didn't worry." Martha came out of the kitchen at that moment and introduced herself to the police.

"We have come to inform you that Mary Quinn was murdered last night."

"Oh my, goodness, murdered where?" cried Martha.

"Her body was found on a ski trail this morning by a group of skiers," said Paine.

"We'd like to view her room to further our investigation into this gruesome crime,"said Clement.

"You are welcome to view her room. Follow me," said Sean.

Evelyn and Harry left the shaken Martha and walked down the hallway to the bedroom. They told Sean they might be awhile as they searched through Mary's belongings in hopes to find evidence and clues to further their investigation. Sean left them and returned to his wife's side to comfort her.

"She was a neat and well organized house guest," said Evelyn Clement. They noticed the bedroom was clean, the bed was made, her clothes were in the dresser and hung up in the closet. They found a shoebox in her closet. They opened it. The box was full of cards sent to her from her parents for birthdays and Christmas. Clement perused the cards, mostly religious ones with messages to continue to follow in the ways of the Lord. There weren't any from admirers or cousins. There was one from her sister, Bridget and one from her brother, Brett. Sean and Martha offered the Mounties a cup of coffee and a freshly baked muffin that Martha had taken from the oven. They agreed to sit in the living room with coffee and muffins and converse about the senseless death.

CHAPTER 5

The staff assembled in the foyer of the Mill River resort. Garth Spencer opened the meeting with the sudden and sad news of the murder of Mary Quinn. The staff all appeared shocked at the news as Trish checked the expressions on their faces. Trish and Charlie and the Freeman twins were given permission to attend the meeting as they were the ones who found the body and would possibly have something to add to the statement.

"How could someone do such a thing?" asked Benny Dorset who appeared distressed and wanted some answers. "Where was the body found?"

Trish spoke up. "My friends and I found the body on a ski trail this morning. The RCMP and EMS took the body to the Prince County Hospital in Summerside where the coroner, Dr. Mack Pathius, will find the cause and time of death."

Kezia Cortez, a housekeeping young woman, started to speak Spanish to Cash Hussain, a kitchen worker who was standing beside her. They whispered to each other as Garth waited for anyone to speak up. Samira Parker nudged Omar Singh to say something.

"This is a tragedy," Omar said.

Rodney Huff was overcome with grief. "Last night Mary asked me if she could get a ride home. I couldn't leave the desk and there was no one here to give her a drive. She decided to hitchhike. Just as she was getting ready to leave, a call came in from an unknown number asking if Mary Quinn had a drive home. Do you think that it was possible the killer was checking on her whereabouts?"

"That's a very strong possibility," said Garth. "Does anyone else have any news to share? Otherwise I think everyone should get back to work."

Trish took John's arm and moved towards Rodney Huff as the crowd started to disperse.

Others wanted to speak to him as well concerning the phone call he had taken last night. Trish and John overheard his repetitive answer that all he knew was what he had already said to the staff that Mary was going to hitchhike home. The thought of having Mary Quinn's cell phone in her pocket weighed heavily on Trish's mind. *If only Paul were here to crack the codes,* she thought.

Rodney was now alone at the front desk and Trish and John had their chance to speak to him. "Hello, Rodney. My name is

Trish Camden and this is John Freeman. We are guests here and we were the ones who found the body of Mary Quinn this morning. I know you've been asked the same question from other staff members but we'd like to know what time the call came in and if you could describe the callers voice?"

"The call came in just after Mary got off work at 6:00 p.m. She had her coat on and was ready to leave. The caller was a man's voice. That's all I know."

"Did you recognize the voice? "No."

"Does the resort have a recording of calls that come in?"

"You'd have to ask Mr. Spencer about that. I don't know."

"Thank you for your time. We'll see you around." "John, let's meet up with Charlie and Josie and make plans for the day. I have something to show you."

They headed back to their rooms and found the other two club members in the Camden's suite. The four of them had cups of hot chocolate while Trish produced the cell phone she had swiped earlier in the morning. "This is Mary Quinn's cell phone."

"How did you get that?" asked Charlie.

"Just a quick slip of the hand when we found the body."

"We need Paul's expertise with cell phones. Did you hear from Paul after you sent a text to him?" asked Charlie.

"No. I sent the text a couple of hours ago. His parents usually give him one of their cars when the CMC need him. I'll text him again to see what he's doing today."

No sooner than Trish re-sent the message, Paul responded, "I'm here."

A knock came at the door. Trish went to answer it. Paul was standing there at the door carrying an overnight bag, some travel munchies, and his faithful laptop. "What took you so long?" teased Trish.

"Just a little drive from Cornwall," said Paul. "Are we ever glad to see you," said Josie. "Having computer problems?"

"We have the cell phone from the dead body. Can you do your magic and find her password?" asked Josie.

"That will be a cinch."

Trish passed the phone to Paul. Within ten minutes he had Mary Quinn's contacts, phone numbers, and address book. "It's all here. The victim has a long list of people that work here, her family, and friends. We've got a great place to start our investigation," said Paul.

CHAPTER 6

The Camden Mystery Club took a team approach to solving the murder. They knew the RCMP would have visited the family by now and probably would have found out what Mary Quinn's address was. They were also likely on their way to Summerside to hear the results of the autopsy from Dr. Mack Pathius and to meet with Staff Sergeant Rob Camden.

Trish began to delegate the tasks. She suggested she and Josie visit the kitchen where Benny Dorset was preparing fresh salads, quiche, and other delectable food for lunch. Then Trish sent Charlie and John to meet Jack Rogers, the activities coordinator. Paul would work independently at his "techy" skills to determine who and where the teams should go next. The CMC said they would meet back at the Camden's suite to discuss their interviews and head to the restaurant for lunch.

Paul settled down to study the contents of the cell phone. He noticed some interesting names and e-mail addresses. Mary's siblings were listed. Her sister, Bridget Quinn and brother, Brett Quinn were on the phone as well as Benny Dorset, Sean and Martha Gallant, and a number of workers at Mill River Resort.

What caught Paul's eye was a friend, Jennifer, with no last name. He found this peculiar, as there were no messages on the phone dating back to 2013, eight years ago. Why would there still be a contact who was not actively communicating with Mary? Where did this Jennifer live? Paul jotted down some notes for the Mystery Club to discuss and continued his search.

Trish and Josie saw the sign, Employees only, on the door to the kitchen. Josie was about to turn away, but signs like this never stopped Trish before; so she tugged Josie to follow her through the doorway into the kitchen. Benny Dorset was busy preparing food for lunch. "I'm sorry, no guests are allowed back here," he said.

"Excuse us. We would like to speak with Benny Dorset. Would that be you?"

"Yes. I'm busy getting three quiches ready for the oven. What do you want?"

"We'd like to ask you a few questions about your friend, Mary Quinn. Josie and I found her body on the ski trail this morning. We belong to a mystery club that solves crimes. My name is Trish. Is there a better time for us to talk with you?"

"If you can wait in the restaurant until I get the quiche in the oven, I'll speak with you for a few minutes. It's getting very close to lunch-time and hotel guests will be coming for lunch."

"Yes. We'll wait for you in the restaurant," said Trish as they went through the exit door.

"Trish, do you have a plan?"

"Josie, we want to ask Benny about his relationship with Mary Quinn. You know, CMC questions."

Benny came through the exit doorway to meet the girls. He wasn't that tall, had short brown hair, wore an apron and glasses, and appeared to be sad when he approached the girls. "I don't have much time, but if you think I can help you solve a senseless crime I would talk to anyone about my girlfriend, Mary."

"When was the last time you saw Mary?" asked Trish.

"We saw each other every day we worked here, briefly of course, as we had different jobs. We just started dating about six months ago. I saw her at the front desk around 5:30 p.m. I couldn't leave the kitchen to drive her home. If only I knew it would be the last time I'd see her alive…Mary was smart and beautiful but lately she was absorbed with anxiety and worries."

"Did she mention she was in danger?"

"No, but she enjoyed our brief relationship and I thought she was unique and special. It is so sad to hear of her death. I can hardly believe it." Benny shook his head and put his face in his hands.

"I know this is hard for you, but, do you know anything about her past, her family?"

"Not really. She said she had a sister who lived in Charlottetown and a brother who lived near here with her parents…Bridget and Brett. She said she had a very religious childhood. That's all I know. I must get back to the kitchen. Good luck with your search. If you have any more questions, I'm usually free at 2:30 p.m. for about an hour."

"Thank you for your time," said Josie. The girls left the restaurant and headed back to the suite.

Charlie and John met Jack Rogers in his office. "Good morning, Mr. Rogers," said Charlie.

"Please call me Jack. What can I do for you?" Jack was young, handsome, and in great physical shape. He wore a jogging suit with the appearance of getting ready for a fitness class.

"We are part of a group called the Camden Mystery Club (CMC) and we were the ones who found Mary Quinn's body earlier today," said John.

"A mystery club? It is extremely sad that Mary Quinn has been murdered. She was like a breath of sunshine most of the time. She always had a smile on her face; so you never got to see behind the outward appearance."

"What time did you see Mary last evening?" asked Charlie.

"I saw her around 6:00 p.m. She was getting ready to leave at the end of her shift. She never asked me for a drive to Alberton. I would have taken her, but she was private. She didn't want to request that of me. I think she was shy around me."

"Do you know her family?"

"I know of them and I dated Mary's sister, Bridget, for a few months before she moved to Charlottetown. Bridget's parents were very strict and religious. They never had a TV. Bridget was looking for an escape from them and found a job in Cornwall. One day she just packed her bags, said good-bye and left. I haven't heard from her since and that would have been a year ago. Mary kept her distance from me. She probably knew my reputation with women. Easy come, easy go. I've dated several women here at Mill River since Bridget has gone." I'm heading out now for a fitness class in the pool.

"One last question. Did Mary have any boyfriends?"

"Just recently she started to date, Benny Dorset, the chef in the kitchen. They seemed to get along. Well, if you'll excuse me I have an 11:30 a.m. class in the pool. It is a sad thing for you to look for leads to find the killer. Good luck." Jack took his clipboard and headed to the pool. Charlie and John went back to the Camden suite to meet up with the rest of the club.

CHAPTER 7

Paul had his eyes glued to the computer screen when the rest of the CMC members arrived back at the Camden suite. "Did you find anything interesting,

Paul? asked Trish. You look fully absorbed in your thoughts."

"Yeah, who is Jennifer? I have a first name with no last name, a cell phone number, and nothing else. It's peculiar. All the other entries on Mary's phone have last names, addresses, and cell phone numbers and there have been fairly recent calls on these phones. Jennifer stands out. There has been no activity on the phone since 2013, eight years ago."

"That does sound odd," said Charlie. "Very unusual," said John.

"Maybe we should try the number and see if it's still active," said Trish.

"I was thinking we should do that, but, wanted to wait until we were all together. Trish, why don't you try the number?"

"OK." Paul handed the phone to Trish so she could dial the number. The person on the cell picked up right away.

"Hello, Mary?" said the voice. "Is this Jennifer?" asked Trish.

"Yes, but you don't sound like Mary Quinn. Who's this?"

"I have Mary's phone. My name is Trish and Mary is dead."

"Dead? How long has she been gone? I haven't spoken to her in a very long time. How did she die?"

"She was murdered here at Mill River Resort last night."

"Oh, no. She was a special friend of mine in high school. This is tragic news. Mary was my first love. I still think of her at times wondering where she is and how she is doing."

"I am deeply sorry for sharing such news. Can you tell me where you live now? After eight years, people lose touch with one another."

"I live and work in Charlottetown and I have a new wife. We are very happy together. I don't think Mary was really gay. I wanted her to be because I was, but back then we just experimented physically with ourselves. I was Mary's first and only friend before she went to Mill River Resort to work. To tell you the truth, I think Mary was fearful anyone would find out about her and me and what we did. She struggled with the lifestyle her parents set as an example for her. They were very strict. I've got to go. My lunch break is almost over. Thank you for telling me about poor Mary. Good-bye." Jennifer shut off her phone.

"You all heard the call. Mary had a deep, dark secret and didn't want anyone to find out about her relationship with Jennifer. Jennifer was Mary's only friend in high school and she was gay and Mary was her first love."

"Let's discuss this over lunch. I'm feeling hunger pangs," said Paul.

They all agreed. At the restaurant they decided to go in Paul's parent's car to Alberton to visit the boarding house where Mary had lived.

Alberton was a small community not far from the resort and it was fairly easy to find Sean and Martha's Boarding House, as it had a sign in the front yard advertising rooms for rent.

The Club met Sean Gallant at the door. "Hello," Trish said. "The five of us belong to a mystery club and found your address as the place where Mary Quinn lived. We are hopeful you will let us come in and see her room for clues to why she was murdered last night."

"The RCMP was already here. You can come into the living room if you like but I will only let the girls go to her room."

"That's OK with us," said Charlie. "We usually don't all come at one time anyway. My name is Charlie Camden. This is John and Paul and the girls are my sister, Trish, and Josie, John's twin sister."

"Come in. Take your boots off at the door. Trish and Josie, you can follow me. Boys, you can sit in there." Sean guided them to the living room and took the girls down the hall. "The Mounties didn't find much, but they didn't tape off the room; so I guess it's OK for you to have a look."

"Thank you, sir."

Trish thought to herself about where Mary would hide something so that nobody would find it. The room was spotless. Her premonitions led her to the bed. She lifted up the mattress from the box spring. As she did, she spied a large brown envelope. Cautiously she picked it up and showed it to Josie. She motioned to Josie not to speak and they replaced the mattress and Trish hid the brown envelope under her coat. They stayed for a few minutes and then left the room and met up with the boys who were chatting with Sean. "Not much luck," Trish said. "Thanks for your hospitality."

The CMC left the house and piled back into Paul's car. "We've got a clue," said Trish. "We found it under the mattress. Let's pull over into a vacant parking lot and have a look."

Paul found a spot to park, shut the engine off and the four of them watched Trish open the envelope with gloves on.

CHAPTER 8

S taff Sergeant Rob Camden, Constable Evelyn Clement, and Corporal Harry Paine met up with Dr. Mack Pathius at the Prince County Hospital. He had just completed the coroner's report.

"The cause of death was strangulation, and the time of death was between 6:30 p.m. and 7:00 p.m." he said. "There were no prints on the body and there was no loss of blood. The victim was choked to death within three to four minutes, as she was deprived of oxygen to the brain."

Retired RCMP officer Coady Freeman waited in the corridor for the news. Once the coroner finished his presentation of details of the death, the Mounties met up with Coady in the hallway and Corporal Paine suggested they find an empty office to give an account of his and Evelyn's news. The unit found a conference room with a table and chairs; so they sat around the table listening for Paine's and Clement's statements.

"First, Constable Evelyn and I departed Mill River Resort and set out for the Quinn family home. We were ushered into the living room by Mrs. Quinn and waited for Mr. Quinn to accompany his wife for our report. They were devastated and grief stricken. David Quinn told us that Mary had a younger sister, Bridget, who lived in Charlottetown and a brother, Brett, who lived at home with them, but he was already at work collecting mussels."

"Violet Quinn, Mary's mother, composed herself enough to tell us where Mary lived in Alberton," said Clement. "We explained as best as we could that Mary's body was at the Prince County Hospital and they were asked to go and identify the body."

"We left the home and went to Alberton to Sean and Martha Gallant's Boarding House."

"They were both home and allowed us to view Mary's bedroom. It was immaculate and after inspecting the entire room the only thing we found was a box of cards that we have in the police car outside, which were sent from Mary's parents dating back to 2013 when

Mary left home."

"Did you find anything suspicious in the box of cards?" asked Rob.

"We didn't examine them fully yet, as we wanted to meet up with you here at the hospital," said Corporal Paine. "The cards were all addressed to Mary Quinn, at Box# 569, Alberton, PE,

C0B 1B0. They were from her parents, one from her sister and one from her brother. They were all very religious."

"Take this evidence back to your office and do a thorough examination of them," said Rob. "Mack, your job is finished. Coady, you and I must head back to the resort and find out what the kids have been up to. This meeting is adjourned."

CHAPTER 9

The Mystery Club members watched Trish open the brown envelope. They knew she was being careful by wearing gloves and not disturbing any possible evidence. She pulled out several envelopes with sheets of white paper, notes that proved Mary Quinn had been blackmailed. The notes were in order, one demanding $1,000 by December 5, the next insisting on a payment of $5,000 by December 12, another ordering $8,000 by January 1, and the final note came demanding $10,000 by January 15, the night she was murdered. Trish read the typed notes to the gang. The notes said that the money must be sent by E-transfer to Rajah345@ hotmail.com. She also found a love letter from Jennifer dating back to 2013.

Dear Mary,   *October 2013*

I think of you often. I miss you. You are a breath of sunshine. I am studying at UPEI and there are no girls that measure up to our special relationship. Do you remember when I first kissed you? I think I caught you by surprise. Our high school years will always be special for me. Please write when you can.

Love,
Jennifer

There was another letter in the brown envelope. Trish opened it. The letter was from a lawyer in Charlottetown. The letter revealed the inheritance money, the sum of $20 000 that would be arriving shortly from the estate of her late Aunt Hilda. Another surprise thought Trish.

"Wow! We've got evidence," Trish exclaimed.

"We've got the blackmail notes but no suspect, yet," said Charlie. "Maybe we should head back to the resort and start further investigation."

"I agree," said Paul as he turned on the engine and the five CMC members headed back to Mill River.

"The envelopes have Mary Quinn's post office box number, #569. How did the blackmailer know this?" asked Trish. "Her parents would know this, as they sent her cards in the mail. Who else would know this box number?"

"I think her immediate family, Jennifer, and anyone she might have told at the resort," said Charlie.

Trish was quiet for a moment. She was staring at the envelope from the lawyer's office. The address on the envelope had her parent's address on it with a forwarding address to her post office number in Alberton. "The lawyer didn't have Mary's box number. The letter was forwarded to her from her family to her post office box number."

"I think we must do our investigations back at the resort," said Paul as he turned on the engine and the club headed for Mill River.

The CMC arrived at the resort. Paul parked the car in the visitor's parking lot and the group decided to split up and interview some of the workers at the inn. They also decided not to mention the contents of the brown envelope to their dads and the Mounties on the case. This was mystery club evidence. Trish and John paired up and Charlie and Josie were a team, which left Paul on his own to study the resort workers' information on the computer.

Kezia and Samira were housekeepers doing the daily cleaning of the rooms. They were about to enter the suite where Paul was using the computer, and were speaking Spanish to each other. They motioned that they'd come back later but Paul said he didn't mind if they cleaned the room while he worked. "We come back later," said Kezia.

"No, it's OK if I stay and work while you clean," said Paul. "Please come in."

The girls entered the room chattering in their mother tongue, thinking Paul didn't understand their language. Paul didn't understand most of what they were saying to each other, but he smiled to himself as they appeared like schoolgirls giggling during their conversation.

CHAPTER 10

Rob and Coady sat in the restaurant having coffee. Barb Freeman was out for a walk and the two men discussed the murder. The waiter overheard their conversation and came over to see if they wanted a menu. "The lunch rush is over but you can still order anything you'd like. I heard you talking about the murder. Mary Quinn was a good friend of mine. My name is Omar and I usually work in the kitchen but at this time of day I wait on tables. Can I get you something?"

"How long have you worked here, Omar?" asked Rob.

"I've been here since 2013, eight years. I was hired the same year that Mary Quinn was hired. We became friends."

"How would you describe her?"

"Mary was very friendly, independent and outgoing. It didn't take long for her to get promotions. I knew her well, but she never talked much about her family. They live close to here and Mary would call and visit them at times but preferred to live at a boarding house in Alberton. She was a good daughter."

"What are your work hours, Omar?" asked Rob.

"I arrive at 6:00 a.m. and work in the kitchen for most of the day. I get off work at 6:00 p.m."

"That's a long day. Do you get any breaks?" "Yes, I get breaks."

"Where do you live?"

"I live in Alberton. Can I get you something?"

"I will have a piece of apple pie. Coady, do you want something?"

"I'll have the same," he replied.

"It is very good. I'll be back in a moment."

"One more person who lives in Alberton," said Rob. "I wonder why he couldn't give Mary a ride last night. He said he gets off work at 6:00 p.m. the same time Mary got off work."

Omar was back with the apple pie. Rob asked, "If you are such good friends with Mary and you both live in Alberton, why couldn't you give her a ride last night?"

Omar looked wary. "I mostly always give Mary drives, but last night I had a date with Samira. She works here, too, and she wanted us to be alone for the first time without my giving Mary a ride home. If only things were normal. Mary would still be here. I feel bad. It's all my fault she was killed last night."

"It's not your fault. Where does Samira work?"

"She works in housekeeping. She is a cleaner. I better see if Benny needs me in the kitchen." Omar excused himself and made his way to the kitchen.

As he was leaving Rob called out to him, "Do you know why anyone would want to kill Mary Quinn?"

Omar turned his head towards the two men and said, "Mary was my friend. I don't know who would do such a thing." Then he disappeared through the doorway into the kitchen.

CHAPTER 11

Violet and David Quinn called their daughter, Bridget, to break the news and she said she'd be home to be with them that night. The couple went to the morgue at the Prince County Hospital to identify the body. This was one of the hardest things they ever had to do and Violet prayed fervently for strength to overcome her raw emotions. Once they knew it was indeed their daughter, they left the morgue and headed for the funeral home to make arrangements for a funeral. They called their church office before leaving for Summerside and by the time they got home there was a steady stream of church members bringing food and offering condolences to the couple. Brett arrived home from work to see a feast of food and to hear the tragedy of the death of his older sister. He didn't like to be around the company of his parent's church goers; so he grabbed some food and headed out until things settled down. Before he left, his mother told him his sister, Bridget, was to come home that evening and she wanted him to be there when she arrived. "I'll be home late. I can't stand this sympathy crap. Got to go. See ya," he said.

David overheard Brett's rude comment to his mother, but, as usual, he let it go as Brett was still a teenager and had to deal with things in his own way. David and Violet had their difficulties with Brett. He had been in trouble with the police before but no charges were ever laid.

CHAPTER 12

Trish and John interviewed Cash Hussain. Cash said he liked Mary and was shocked by her death. He didn't have a car and lived within walking distance of the resort. He also said he worked from 8:00 a.m. until 8:00 p.m. He was always greeted by Mary in the mornings when he'd come in for work in the kitchen. When Mary took her breaks quite often, she would come into the galley for a visit with Benny, Omar, and him. She'd get a treat from Benny, usually a croissant, and would have a tea while they were busy preparing meals for guests. Trish asked about the housekeeping staff and this request startled the three cooks. They didn't associate with the workforce away from the kitchen. Trish was puzzled by this information and tucked it away in her photographic memory bank. John and Trish saw their dads in the restaurant; so they went to sit with them.

"How are things going with you, two?" asked Trish's dad.

"We're meeting some of the employees," said Trish. "How about you?"

"We spoke with Omar Singh and he had kind words about Mary. He also said he couldn't drive Mary home from work last night, as he was going on a date with Samira, a housekeeper here at the resort."

"Really? We just came from the kitchen and it was my impression that the kitchen staff didn't associate with the housekeeping staff," said Trish.

"Well, Coady, you heard Omar say that, didn't you?"

"Yes, he said he usually drove Mary home, but Samira wanted the two of them to have a night alone."

"Interesting," said Trish. "I think we must do more investigation with the housekeeping staff."

"By the way, did you find anything in Alberton at the boarding house this morning?" asked Rob.

"Nothing significant," lied Trish. She hated to lie to her father but wanted some time to reflect on the contents of the brown envelope with the Club members. "We will see you later for dinner."

"We have a reservation for 6:30 p.m. Don't be late," said Rob.

"We won't. See you later." Trish gave a little wave and the two of them were off. "I think we should check in with Paul and see if he has heard anything from Charlie and Josie."

"OK, you're in the lead," said John.

Paul was munching on some treats he had brought from home when Trish and John arrived at the suite. "Hi," said Paul.

"Hey, Paul, what's new?" asked Trish.

"While you guys were gone, two of the housekeeping women were here. They spoke to each other in Spanish. I asked them if they heard of the murder. The one with the name, Kezia, on her name label, said, 'No good English. We know nothing.' The other one, Samira, said, 'murder is sad,'". Paul then explained to Trish and John that he sensed they knew more English than they said they did. "They saw the brown envelope on the desk with the name, Mary Quinn, on it and they appeared nervous and spoke to each other while glancing at the envelope. Then they left in a hurry. It all seemed odd."

"It does sound strange," said Trish. "We met up with Dad and Coady Freeman at the restaurant and they told us that Omar Singh almost always drives Mary home, but last night Samira and Omar had a date which left Mary without a drive. Why would the kitchen staff say they didn't associate with the cleaning workers when Omar and Samira went on a date? Someone is lying. Why?"

"It sounds as if more than one person knows something about the murder," said Paul.

"Have you heard from Charlie and Josie?" asked Trish.

"They were here about a half hour ago. They interviewed Rodney Huff, the Jamaican, at the front desk. Charlie said he appeared to be confused about the cell call that came in last night when Mary Quinn was about to leave the resort. The more he thought of it the more he thought it could have been the killer wanting to know if Mary had a ride home. Mary left just after the call came in."

"Is there any way a call like that can be traced, Paul?" asked Trish.

"It's highly unlikely that the cell phone of the killer would be his own phone, but I think the call can be traced with a warrant and we can go to the phone company that is the provider. It could be a burner phone that can't be traced back to the person using it. Anyway, Charlie and Josie went for a swim and sauna and said to join them in the pool if there was time. Do you guys want to go for a swim before supper?"

"I'd like to try the water slide," said John. "OK. Paul, are you coming?"

"Yes."

The three CMC members joined up with the two in the pool. They had an intense day and spent some time relaxing.

CHAPTER 13

November

Mary Quinn had a lot of respect for her boss, Garth Spencer. That is why she trusted him to help her understand the letter she just received from a Charlottetown lawyer. She went to him to ask his advice. "Garth, I would like your opinion. I have a letter that I got in the mail yesterday from a lawyer in Charlottetown who writes I have inherited $20 000 from an Aunt Hilda whom I have never met. Would you please have a look?"

"Certainly, Mary," Garth said. Garth took the letter, made a copy for himself and reviewed the letter with Mary. "It does indeed look as if you will be receiving the sum of money in the mail soon. Congratulations, Mary. You deserve a break like this."

Mary thanked Garth and left his office with the original letter in her possession. Smiling to herself, she went back to the front desk and resumed her duties. Garth Spencer was happy for his employee, but carelessly left his copy of the letter on his office desk. He went about his work when the Spanish housekeeping, young woman, Kezia, came in to clean the office. She spied the letter on her boss' desk and read its contents. When she left, she made a mental note of the sum of money Mary was to inherit. As is human nature to spread gossip, Kezia told her friend Samira, who told Omar, who informed the kitchen staff, Benny and Cash, and the news of Mary's inheritance made its way around the entire staff. No one approached Mary about the news they received.

Brett Quinn, at nineteen, made regular visits to the bar at the resort for a drink after a long, tiresome day at work. He needed to get out of the house where he lived with his parents. Like his sisters before him, he was looking for a way to move out of the house and be independent of his parents. Money was the big issue; he never seemed to have enough of it. One evening after Mary had left for her boarding house in Alberton, Brett was at the bar having a few drinks with another staff member. He was feeling the effects of the booze and began talking. "My oldest sister, Mary, had a love affair with a girl, Jennifer, in high school before she started working here. It was a long time ago; Jennifer left and went to UPEI. I think that was the last of their relationship. I was young at the time, but I used to see them kissing and hugging. They were a regular couple."

"Really, a love affair, I never knew this about Mary," said the staff member. "Brett, you've had enough to drink. I think you'd better head out. The bar is about to close."

The staff member helped Brett to his feet and escorted him to the door. "Sleep it off and get to work tomorrow."

Brett's confidant began plotting ways he could get Mary's money.

CHAPTER 14

Constable Evelyn Clement and Corporal Harry Paine started the next day with fresh eyes. They perused the box of cards that they confiscated from the boarding house. They decided to interview the sister, Bridget, and the brother, Brett. The detectives knew Bridget had arrived to be with her parents. Constable Clement and Corporal Paine met both Bridget and Brett at the Quinn residence, Sunday morning. Then they spent some time interviewing resort employees. They found out that Mary had inherited money from Mary's dead aunt. This was motive for blackmail. They continued to report to Staff Sergeant Rob Camden the results of their findings.

It was a mild day. It had rained during the night. The sun was out and glistened off the melting snow. It was an early rise for Trish, as she knew the weekend would be over and the Club members would be heading back to their homes in Cornwall. She had to find the killer today. Where were her premonitions telling her to go? She didn't want to disturb her family. She crept out of her bed, dressed in the bathroom and headed out for a morning escapade. She wanted to go back to the sight where the body lay on the snow. She wanted to take another look at the crime scene. She hiked down the driveway and on to the trail. Enough snow had melted during the night to expose a very different view of the scene she had seen yesterday. She saw something sparkling in the snow. She bent down and picked it up. It was a gold chain with a symbol of a Taoist yin yang on it. She recognized the symbol for male and female, black and white with a swirling, opposite design. The chain was broken. It must have fallen off the killer in a struggle for Mary to save her life. What a find! How many people wore a gold chain with a yin yang on it? This piece of evidence would solve the felony. Excitedly Trish headed back to the resort to share her find with the Mystery Club members.

She found the families in the restaurant. "Good morning, Trish," said Dad. "You were up early. Did you go for a walk?"

"Yeah, I couldn't sleep." She wasn't going to share her findings with the adults in the room. Paul looked at Trish who winked at him. He knew this was a sign of something she had found.

"I think the Club members should head back to the room," Paul said. They had just sat down when Trish arrived, and they hadn't had anything to eat. For Paul to say this was unusual, as he was such a hearty eater who loved his food. Charlie caught Trish's eye and knew something was up. He stood up and the twins got up and they all excused themselves saying they'd eat some of the food they brought from home for breakfast. The Freemans and Rob were left alone.

"Something is up. Trish must have done something or found something for them to all leave at once," said Rob.

Coady and Barb agreed. "I hope they aren't getting into something dangerous," said Barb.

The CMC closed the door behind them back at the Camden suite. Trish could hardly contain her excitement. "I found a significant clue at the site of the murder this morning when I went for a walk. It's a gold chain with a yin yang pendant on it. It must have fallen off the murderer as Mary Quinn was struggling to get free. Now all we need to find out is who around here wore a yin yang symbol on a gold chain."

"Show us the necklace," said John.

"Here, have a look." Trish pulled the chain out of her pocket with a kleenex.

The Club members all wanted to pass it around but Charlie stopped them when he said, "this is evidence and we shouldn't put our fingerprints on it."

They all agreed. "Well, we can get started by going in the same pairs we had yesterday with the gold chain and yin yang and visiting some of the hotel workers. We'll have to take turns using our gloves and making our way around the staff," said Trish as she reached for her gloves.

"This is such a find," said Josie.

"Do you think anyone is going to rat on one of their co-workers?" asked Paul.

"When it comes to murder, I think they will," said Trish.

"Well, I'll stay here while you and John visit some of the kitchen staff and Charlie and Josie can go back to see the front desk workers," said Paul. "You'll have to take turns, as only one pair at a time will have the yin yang with them."

"Let's go," said Trish.

"Don't you want to eat something first?" asked John.

"Oh, yeah, I forgot." Trish downed a muffin and a cup of tea. Now she was ready to spring into action. John accompanied her leaving the others to have a more leisurely breakfast. They headed for the kitchen. The employee's only sign didn't stop Trish's exuberance. She boldly pushed the door open and was halted by Benny Dorset.

"You can't come in here. We are very busy serving breakfast," said Benny sternly.

"It's very important, Benny. We have evidence that could lead us to the killer of your girlfriend."

"Right now is not a good time. Come back at 10:00 a.m. I must insist. Now please go."

"Trish, we'd better go," said John.

"We'll be back at 10:00," said Trish as they left. "We may as well let Charlie and Josie have the necklace and let them follow up with their investigation. Let's go back to the room."

Disappointed, Trish and John returned to the suite and gave the pendant to Charlie. "Don't forget we have a date with the kitchen staff at 10:00 a.m.; so don't be late."

"We won't."

Charlie and Josie left with surgical gloves and the precious yin yang symbol in their possession. They met Rodney Huff at the front desk. He was friendly and remembered them from yesterday. "You two, again, how can I help you?"

"We were wondering if you have ever seen anyone here at Mill River Resort wearing this pendant?" asked Josie.

"That is a very familiar- looking symbol. I have seen it before but never on anyone here at the resort. Do you think it has some link to the killer?"

"That is what we thought. It was found at the crime scene this morning," said Charlie.

"Sorry, I can't be of more help. Maybe the housekeeping staff might know of someone wearing it," said Rodney.

"Thanks for your help." Charlie and Josie checked the time. They had an hour; so they went to see a couple of young women who worked in housekeeping. They went searching for the two girls Paul had mentioned that were cleaning the suite when he was in the room yesterday. They found them in a room not too far from the Camden suite changing bedding.

"Good morning. Are you Kezia and Samira?" asked Charlie.

"Yes, I am Kezia." "I am Samira."

"Do you recognize this necklace? Who wore this necklace?"

"English not good. Necklace? Who wear this? I don't know," said Kezia.

"I don't know," repeated Samira.

They exchanged glances and began speaking in their own language. "Sorry," said Kezia, "We must clean rooms."

"Thank you," said Charlie.

"Well, we didn't get too far. Hopefully, Trish and

John will make more progress," said Josie as they headed for the rooms.

By the time they met Trish, John, and Paul, it was getting close to ten. Trish asked, "Any luck?"

"We saw Rodney Huff at the front desk. He didn't know anyone with that chain and pendant. Then we went to see the housekeepers, Kezia and Samira. They didn't have anything to say to us, but they looked at each other quizzically and then began speaking in Spanish," said Charlie.

"I think they may be hiding something from us," said Josie.

"They looked kind of suspicious to me, too," said Charlie.

"We'll get to the bottom of this," said Trish. "Are you ready, John?"

"Let's go," he said.

Trish and John left at precisely 10:00 a.m. to visit the kitchen crew. Benny was in a much more amiable mood. Trish had the chain and yin yang in a plastic bag in her pocket. The two entered the kitchen to meet up with Omar, Cash, and Benny. "I see it is a good time for you to ask your questions," said Benny.

"We want to know how the blackmailer knew of the money Mary Quinn inherited?" asked Trish completely on speculation and premonition. "We know she was being blackmailed. We have proof of this. Who knew this about her?"

"Everybody knew she inherited $20 000," said Omar. "It was the gossip of the workers here at the resort."

"Who started the rumour?" asked John.

"I heard it from Samira who heard it from Kezia. Kezia saw a letter in Garth's office from a lawyer," said Omar.

"I heard that the housekeepers didn't have anything to do with the kitchen crew," said Trish. "Who told this lie?"

Omar was caught. He didn't want the others to know about Samira and him. He said, "I told that lie to the men in the restaurant yesterday. I didn't want anyone to know about Samira and me."

"Why?" asked Trish.

"You see, it doesn't look good for the staff to interact socially. Samira wanted to go on a date with me. We decided to go on Friday night. That is why I couldn't drive Mary home. Samira is jealous of Kezia. Kezia has very good English; that is why she read the letter in Mr. Spencer's office. Kezia has a boyfriend who lives near the resort. His name is Brett Quinn, Mary Quinn's brother."

Trish couldn't believe all this information was coming to a head. Suddenly she pulled the yin yang out of her pocket. "Do any of you recognize this chain and pendant? Is it yours, Omar?"

"No. I've never seen it before," he said. "Is it yours, Cash?" asked Trish.

"No. It's not mine."

"Benny, who owns this chain and symbol?" asked Trish.

"Where did you find it?" Benny asked. "At the crime scene," said Trish.

CHAPTER 15

"It belonged to Mary," said Benny. "She kept it hidden under her clothes and didn't want anyone to see it. I knew of it because she showed it to me when we were dating. It must have fallen off when she was murdered."

"Who was blackmailing, Mary?" asked Trish. "And why did Kezia pretend to have poor English when she was able to read the letter from the lawyer which was in Garth Spencer's office?"

The three cooks from the kitchen looked at one another. They didn't know who was blackmailing Mary. They didn't know why she was murdered. Omar knew Kezia had a boyfriend, Brett Quinn. This much they did know. Now Trish knew this as well.

"Omar, you said Brett and Kezia are a couple. Do you think Brett could have killed his own sister?" asked Trish.

"I don't know Brett. He comes into the resort in the evenings sometimes to have a drink. I usually get off work at 6:00 p.m.;

so I don't see him in the evenings. Cash works until 8:00 p.m. Have you seen him here in the evenings, Cash?"

"Yes. Sometimes he has too much to drink. He drinks alone most of the time. There was one night when I was serving him last November when Jack Rogers was drinking with him. He was drunk and Jack told him he had had enough and sent him home. That was the only time I ever saw him with anyone. I knew he had a thing for Kezia. They would leave the bar together most nights."

"Jack Rogers, the activities director?" asked Trish.

"Yeah, they were buddies for a night last November.

Never saw them together again."

Trish was processing the news. *The first blackmail letter that arrived demanded $1000 by December 5, 2020. It left just enough time for someone to know about the inheritance and get the scoop about the affair with*

Jennifer. If Brett didn't send the letters, maybe Jack Rogers did. If it were Jack Rogers, what was his motive? How did he get Mary's postal box number?

John and Trish thanked the kitchen staff. They knew they had spent enough time with them, as the crew had to get back to work. "We have more questions to discuss with the rest of the Club," said Trish.

"I agree with you there, Trish."

The CMC met up in the Camden suite with Trish bubbling with news. "John and I have some baffling news to share. One, the blackmail letters could have been written by Brett, Mary's younger brother, or by Jack Rogers, the activities coordinator. We also found out that Kezia speaks very good English. That is why she was able to read the legal letter on Garth Spencer's desk and start the rumour about Mary's inheritance. She is the girlfriend of Brett Quinn. The puzzle pieces keep coming together. Another thing we found out was the gold chain and pendant belonged to Mary, not the killer. Benny knew this and admitted it."

"Whoa, Trish. Let's think about what you've just uncovered," said Paul. "The blackmail letters, you say, could have been written by Brett Quinn or by Jack Rogers. I can see that Brett would easily be able to find out Mary's postal box number, but how would Jack Rogers find this out?"

"That's been one of my questions. The inheritance money must have been an incentive for someone to blackmail Mary, and someone must have had a humongous grudge on her to actually kill her. Brett Quinn or Jack Rogers could be involved and don't forget Kezia, as she lied about her lack of English. Maybe she is in cahoots with Brett," said Trish.

Josie listened intently. "Jack Rogers seems so friendly, handsome and genuinely nice. How could he possibly be the killer?" she asked. "We've never met Brett Quinn; so I don't know about his character."

"Don't be fooled by a handsome face, Josie," said Charlie. "I think it is time to share some of our knowledge with the detectives on the case."

"Charlie, are you crazy? We've got the brown envelope, we know about Kezia and Brett, we know about the gold chain, we know about Jack and Brett sharing a few drinks together prior to the blackmail letters. Do you honestly think we should give the investigative information up at this stage in the game?"

"All I'm saying is maybe they have information about Brett that we don't have, Trish."

"We can live without that info for now. Right now we have to find more of a motive than $20 000. The person killing Mary had a horrible grudge upon her and we have to find out who and why that grudge came to be."

"How do you suppose we can find that out, Trish?" asked Charlie.

"Well, for starters, I think we need to interview both Brett and Jack. Today is Sunday and Brett should have the day off; so two of us can meet him and then two of us can question Jack Rogers. I'd like to have a conversation with Brett and John can come with me. Charlie, you and Josie can talk with Jack Rogers."

"What is the primary question we want to ask?" said John.

"Oh, John, we've been doing this for a long time.

We wing it," said Trish.

CHAPTER 16

Charlie did not pressure Trish into consulting with the detectives on the case; so he and Josie went to the office of the recreation coordinator. Jack wasn't in his office. It was Sunday and they wondered if he had the day off. They spoke with the unknown receptionist at the front desk and found out that Jack would be in by 1:00 p.m. They also were in contact with their parents. Check-out time for the weekend was noon. This complicated matters. Charlie pleaded the case that his father leave the resort and head back to Cornwall with the Freemans and leave the car for Trish and him to drive back later that day. Rob wasn't too happy about this arrangement, but Coady and Barb would give him a drive. Josie and John were to stay with the CMC to follow up on their investigation. All was established. Trish and John were to visit the Quinn home, Josie and

Charlie were to meet up with Jack Rogers at 1:00 p.m. and Paul had to spend his time in the restaurant with his laptop. He didn't mind this arrangement as long as he could have his fill of munchies.

Trish and John walked to the Quinn residence. An old truck was in the yard, but no other vehicles. Trish knocked on the door. Then John knocked on the door. No answer. They both knocked on the door and a noise was heard. They waited. A young man opened the door.

"Are you Brett Quinn?" Trish asked. "Yeah, what do you want?" he said.

"We heard about your sister, Mary. We are sorry for your loss. Can we talk to you for a minute?"

"What's this about?"

"My name is Trish Camden and this is John Freeman. We belong to a mystery club and…"

"Whoa. I already talked to the Mounties this morning. I have nothing else to say."

Brett was just about to slam the door in their faces when Trish piped up and said, "We know about the blackmail letters and we know about the inheritance that Mary received. We'd just like to talk."

"What are you talking about? Blackmail letters? Are you accusing me of sending blackmail letters to Mary? How would I go about that? I'd like to know," said Brett belligerently.

"Well, you could have sent them to her post office box in Alberton, threatening her to pay up and when the last letter was sent and she didn't follow up with the payment, you snuck over to the resort knowing what time she got off work and you killed her."

"You are crazy. I don't get off work until six and then I have to drive home. I'm not even home until close to seven. I knew about the inheritance money, but you guys have the wrong guy," said Brett.

"If what you are saying is true, who else knows about Mary's past relationship with Jennifer?"

"I don't know. It was a long time ago. I may have mentioned it to someone at the bar in the resort. I was drunk and this guy sent me home. I can't remember his name. Jennifer and Mary had a gay relationship. I used to see them together hugging and kissing. This confused me as a child. My parents never knew."

"Where are your parents?" asked John.

"They go to church on Sundays. I did not blackmail my sister."

"What do the detectives know? Why did they interview you?"

"I'm going back to bed. It's my day off. No further questions." And with that he slammed the door on Trish and John.

Charlie and Josie waited with Paul in the restaurant where they had lunch. At 1:00 p.m. they left Paul and went to see Jack Rogers. Jack was openly friendly, was physically fit, and invited them into his office where he kept gym equipment.

"What can I do for you?" he asked.

"We heard about the death of Mary Quinn and wondered how well you knew her?"

"That's a sad story. I didn't know Mary very well. She wasn't a girl I could flirt with, if you know what I mean," said Jack.

"Did you know about her inheritance?" asked Charlie.

"That rumour spread fast. Everyone knew about her inheritance."

"Who started the rumour?" asked Josie.

"It started with the housekeeping girls, I think," said Jack as he began to feel tension throughout his body.

"Where were you Friday night when Mary got off work?"

"Why ask the question? I was here as usual."

"We know of blackmail letters sent to Mary since the beginning of December. Do you know who would have sent them?" asked Charlie.

Suddenly, Jack got red in the face. He moved towards the two teenagers, grabbed Charlie and put him in a headlock and said in a not so friendly voice, "How did you find those letters?" Josie tried to kick Jack but Jack gave Josie a Judo kick to the stomach and knocked the wind out of her and she fell to the floor. He was so strong he tied Charlie up and dragged Josie into a standing position and tied her up as well using skipping ropes. The ropes were skin-tight. Jack led them towards the pool area. No one was at the pool. No one saw them. Jack marched them into the sauna and taking more ropes he tied their feet together and placed gags in their mouths. Charlie and Josie were left in the heat of the sauna fully clothed and trapped! Jack left them there and returned to his office to scheme his next move. Murder once, now he had to dispose of the two nosey teenagers.

Paul met up with Trish and John at the restaurant. "Have you seen Charlie and Josie?" asked Trish.

"They went to ask Jack Rogers some questions at one o'clock. That was an hour ago. I haven't seen them. They should have come back by now," said Paul.

"Something's wrong," said Trish tingling with premonitions. "Paul, if John and I don't come back within thirty minutes, call 911 and get the RCMP to come. We think Jack Rogers is the killer."

Trish and John headed for Jack Rogers office. Jack appeared edgy when they met him. Trish and John asked him if he saw

Charlie and Josie, but he said no. He hadn't seen anyone since he arrived at work. Trish knew he was lying. What had he done with them? Where would a recreation coordinator dispose of the bodies? Trish was in panic mode. Trish didn't want the killer to capture her and John; so, they thanked him and left. Trish was scared. Where were Charlie and Josie? John suggested they head back to see Paul in the restaurant.

Charlie sucked on the gag in his mouth trying to loosening it. Josie was doing the same thing. The gag became wet and Charlie used his tongue to push it free from his mouth. He spoke to Josie. "Keep on relaxing and slackening the gag from your mouth, Josie."

Finally she got it loose. "It sure is hot in here," were her first words.

"If we sit back to back maybe we can untie the ropes around our hands," said Charlie.

They maneuvered their bodies so they could try to undo the knots on their hands. It required patience and skill, both of which they had a lot of. Eventually they loosened the rope around Charlie's fingers and he was released from the bond. Quickly he untied Josie's hands and then they both freed their feet. They opened the door of the sauna and were relieved from the warm pool air. "How are we going to get out of here without Jack Rogers seeing us?" asked Josie.

"We have to make it back to the restaurant and find Paul. Trish and John are probably with him by now. We've got to call the RCMP."

Charlie and Josie carefully made their way, undetected by Jack Rogers, to the restaurant. Trish hugged her brother. John hugged his sister. Paul called the Mounties. Jack Rogers arrived at the restaurant and found the Club members with Paul using his cell phone. He flew at Paul, but Paul saw him coming. He diverted away from Jack and finished the call.

Jack Rogers was furious. He said, "You are a bunch of pesky little teenagers. You haven't any evidence of anything and I'll deny everything."

"What's going on here?" asked Garth Spencer, the resort manager as he entered the restaurant and saw Jack in an unusual state of fury.

"Jack Rogers tied us up and gagged Josie and me and left us in the sauna. We could have died in there," said Charlie.

"Jack, why did you do this?"

"Those kids are nosey and I did no such thing.

They are lying."

CHAPTER 17

The RCMP arrived and put handcuffs on Jack Rogers. Constable Evelyn Clement and Corporal Harry Paine stayed with the CMC to listen to their spokeswoman, Trish Camden, disclose the evidence in the brown envelope: the blackmail letters, the letter from Jennifer, and the letter from the lawyer about

Mary Quinn's inheritance.

"You can't pin this on me," said Jack. "You have no proof of my involvement in this murder."

"You will come with us to the RCMP station for questioning," said Corporal Paine to Jack Rogers, "And your Club better make its way to the station as well to confirm the evidence."

"We'll do that sir," said Trish.

The CMC knew that they didn't have definite proof to convict Jack Rogers of murder. They consulted one another about this as they left the resort and went to the RCMP headquarters. The

Camdens and Freemans were in one car and talked amongst themselves, but realized they needed Paul's expertise with his computer skills to trace the previous history on Jack's life. Paul drove his parent's car. The Camdens, Freemans and Paul all arrived at the same time. Before they entered the police station Trish asked Paul to do a background check on Jack Rogers.

The Club knew their way around a police station, but this office was different from the one in Charlottetown. It was much smaller. The two RCMP officers placed Jack Rogers in an interviewing room while they escorted the CMC into another. First and foremost, the two detectives were displeased at the Club for not sharing the evidence they had found in the brown envelope. "How long have you had the evidence you found in the brown envelope and where the heck did you find it?" asked Paine in a perturbed voice.

"We found it between the mattress and the box spring in Mary Quinn's bedroom at the Gallant's Boarding House in Alberton," said Trish.

"We didn't look there," said Clement.

"This information has blackmail letters, typed and dated back to the first one wanting $1000 by December 5th in an E-transfer money to Rajah345@hotmail. com . The other three letters escalate in amounts of money the blackmailer wants from $5000 to $8000 to $10 000 by January 15th," said Paine. "We found out about the inheritance money Mary received;

so we presume the blackmailer knew this as well. Do you have anything else we should know before we interview this man in the next room?"

"Charlie and I were taken as hostages, tied up, gagged, and left in the sauna at the resort. It was terribly hot in there and we were just lucky we escaped when we did or maybe we would have died," said Josie.

"This is the only proof we have on Jack Rogers," said Paine. "Is there anything else we can convict him for?"

Paul was researching on his laptop about Jack Rogers and just found something interesting. "Jack Rogers was married once before and had a child. The marriage ended tragically, as he beat up his wife leaving her with permanent scars to her face. She was terrified of him and refused to press charges; however, he has had to pay child support and this inheritance money would have helped with that," he said.

"This is good support for a case," said Corporal Paine. "Your Club must wait here while Constable Clement and I speak with the suspect."

The two RCMP offices closed the door to the room holding the Mystery Club members and opened the other door to see Jack Rogers seated at a table and with handcuffs on his wrists resting on the table.

"We have quite a lot of information stacked up against you, Jack Rogers," said Corporal Paine as he entered the room and sat across from him while Constable Evelyn stood close by.

Face to face Jack Rogers didn't look like the upbeat, positive, friendly, recreation coordinator at the resort. This afternoon he looked just like any other convict waiting for his chance to plead his innocence. "I am not guilty," he said.

"We have testimony from two persons that you tied them up, gagged them, and left them to die in the sauna at the Mill River Resort. These witnesses can testify and their pleas will stand up in court."

"I did what I had to do, but I am not guilty of any other charges you may have against me."

"What I'd like to know is why you did such a horrendous thing in the first place?"

"I know my rights. I want a lawyer."

"You think you can just call up a lawyer and presto you are freed? It would take time for a lawyer to come from Summerside and we don't have any local lawyers here. Why don't you cooperate and explain your motive in carrying out such an appalling act?"

"Look, those kids provoked me." "How?"

Jack thought for a moment. "Those kids said they knew about the blackmail letters sent to Mary Quinn. How in heck did they know this?"

"Are you confessing you sent the letters to Mary Quinn? Are you confessing that when she didn't pay any more you killed her?"

"No, no, no! I am not confessing anything. I want a lawyer before I say another word."

"You are just prolonging the agony. You may get a lawyer," said Paine.

The detectives left the suspect. They returned with a cell phone and a list of attorneys. Jack made a call. The legal representative would be there in an hour.

The Mystery Club members knew this was going to be a dragged-out affair. Waiting was not one of Trish's favourite things to do. She wanted things to happen immediately. It would be dark soon and they had to get back home, as they had school the next day.

The detectives entered the room with the Club members. "I just spoke with your dad, Trish and Charlie. He said he wants you home tonight; so, you might as well give us the brown envelope you confiscated from Mary Quinn's bed. We'll need to look at it and then send it to Charlottetown tomorrow to have it checked for fingerprints on the letters. We can handle everything else here. Your Club has done some very good work," said Corporal Paine.

Trish, wearing gloves as protocol, reluctantly gave up the evidence. "We'd like you to keep us posted on the case. I guess we'd better leave. He's guilty. The fingerprints will prove it," she said.

CHAPTER 18

"I'll ride with Paul. Charlie, you can take John and Josie with you," Trish said to the gang in the parking lot of the RCMP station. It was time to head home. Paul suggested they stop in Kensington for Chinese food at a local restaurant for supper. Trish, Charlie, and the twins all chuckled at Paul, as he always had his timed dinners lined up; so they agreed with him.

"Why would any woman stay married to a man like Jack when the abuse was so bad? I would never do that," said Trish to Paul in the car on their way to Kensington.

"You don't know what other factors were involved. They had a child. He could have brainwashed her. You just see things from the outside, Trish. You can't see what happens behind closed doors. Remember she did leave him in the end and he has to pay child support."

"Did you get any more information about her on the computer? Her name, for instance?"

"Her name was not revealed in the news release. Probably she was too scared of him to have her name printed with the article."

"Changing the subject, do you agree with me that Jack Rogers is Mary Quinn's killer?"

"Yes, I do. The evidence has to prove it, though. We'll have to wait on that. Your dad will keep you informed and the detectives in Charlottetown, Sergeant Frank Brown and Corporal Kurt Lewis, will be on the case of fingerprints on the blackmail letters."

They were silent for a while. Trish was thinking about Mary Quinn. She never got to meet her parents. She never got to tell them how sorry she was. The funeral would be this week. She'd like to go, but, it was a long drive to Alberton, she had school, and Dad wouldn't approve of her missing school. *There were so many things not resolved,* she thought. "How did Jack Rogers get Mary Quinn's post office box number in Alberton?" she blurted out.

"That's a good question. He must have sneaked a glance at her employment file at the resort."

"Yeah, that's a question for the Mounties to ask in the interrogation room."

They pulled into the restaurant parking lot with Charlie and the twins behind them. Trish was contemplative as the group were ushered to a table. Once their orders were placed, she decided to share what was on her mind. "Why did Kezia and Samira always seem to be suspicious? What connection to the murder did Kezia play, if any? And why did she pretend to have poor English when, in fact, she could read a legal letter? What did her relationship with Brett Quinn have to do with the case?"

"Slow down, Trish. One question at a time," said Charlie. "You need to be the one interrogating Jack Rogers. Did you get a cell phone number for one of the Mounties so you could ask these questions for their interview?"

"It's funny you are saying that. As a matter of fact I did get Evelyn's cell number at the RCMP station. She is a new detective and didn't seem to know protocol. She slipped it to me on a piece of paper without Corporal

Harry Paine noticing. I can text her questions for her to ask the suspect."

"That's great, Trish," said Josie.

Trish began sending texts while they waited for their food to arrive. "Evelyn says the lawyer, Carmen Stoke, has arrived. They are just about to start the interview with Carmen and Jack. Then she says she'll ask whatever I text her to ask. What do you think we should ask first?"

"Ask about the relationship Brett Quinn had with Jack Rogers," said Paul, "and what relationship Brett Quinn had with Kezia Cortez."

Trish sent the text. The food arrived before she got a response. "Brett and Jack knew each other as they would share a drink at the bar." Trish was elaborating verbally about the text message, as it was in brief, fragmented grammar. "She also says Brett and Kezia have been a couple for the last six months."

Trish sent another text. In between waiting for a response she nibbled her food. "Kezia planted the seed of the idea for Brett to get Mary's inheritance. Kezia knew about the secret Mary had about Jennifer because

Brett told her," Trish said. Trish texted back, "Find out who planned the blackmail."

Evelyn's response came, "Kezia and Jack."

The Club members were shocked that Kezia and Jack were in cahoots with each other.

"Can you believe it?" exclaimed Trish. "Kezia and Jack. Brett had nothing to do with the blackmail letters." Trish began to text Evelyn again. It said, "Did you get a confession from Jack about the murder of Mary Quinn?"

The response came. "Jack confessed. Yes, he murdered Mary for the money."

"Will you bring Kezia in for aiding and abetting the murder?" was Trish's next text.

"Yes," was the response.

The Club finished their meal conversing about the case and the turn of events.

At home that night, Trish spoke to her father about the case. "The murder was committed by Jack Rogers. He admitted it. Kezia Cortez will be charged with aiding and abetting Jack for the murder. I'm going to call Constable Evelyn Clement to ask a few questions about the interview and see if the Mounties have Kezia in custody."

"It didn't take you very long to solve this mystery, Trish," said Rob.

"What happens to the money that Jack and Kezia acquired from Mary?" asked Trish.

"The courts will probably tell them they have to pay it back to the estate of Mary Quinn."

Trish was on the cell phone. When she got off the phone, she said, "Dad, Corporal Paine and Constable Clement brought Kezia into custody. She was the initiator and instigator behind the whole scheme. Jack's lawyer advised him to plead guilty. There will be a court hearing for them both. It's been quite a weekend."

BOOK 6:

BASIN HEAD
BAD BOYS

CHAPTER 1

The most exciting place to go for a thrill if you are a teenager is bridge jumping at Basin Head in Prince Edward Island. It has always been the excitement of the Camden Mystery Club to make it to Basin Head for the exhilarating adventure. This year, however, there were security guards posted around the wharf and bridge, preventing anyone from jumping due to shallow water and the risks of injuries and possible death. The Club members did not know about this ruling from July of 2020 and were disappointed with the news.

"Well, we can still go swimming and we've brought wood so we can have a campfire," said Trish. "Paul, you did bring food, didn't you?"

"As always, Trish."

Charlie met up with some of his university friends; so he disappeared from the Club members for awhile. It was early evening when they arrived in two cars, the old 2005 Camden Toyota which Charlie drove, and Paul's parent's car, a Nissan. John and Josie, the Freeman twins came with Paul. They had their swim while Trish noticed teens trying to sneak a jump from the wharf which wasn't as well guarded as the bridge. They decided to have their campfire on the left-hand side of the bridge on the 'singing sands' beach. They were called 'singing sands' because people who walked on the beach made a noise on the sand with their feet. The Club members had summer jobs, John and Josie at Cows on the North River causeway, Paul with a computer company, Charlie at the university sociology department, and Trish at Pizza Delight in Cornwall. This trip to Basin Head was once a summer and they had to coordinate all their work schedules to plan this outing.

Paul got the food organized and the Club settled down for a late supper after their swim. "I wonder where Charlie is? It isn't like him to miss a meal," said Trish.

"I saw him drinking with some of his buddies. He'll be back when it's time to go home," said Josie.

The four of them ate and sat around the campfire. The sun was setting on the horizon with golden, orange, and red hues of colour displayed which eventually turned to indigo and purple at twilight and the first sight of stars in the night sky. The security guards left for the night and many teens were gone as well. Trish noticed a group of five teens on the wharf playing what looked like some sort of game. The tide was out and the party of friends started dancing and prancing around each other. Trish mentioned the group to the other Club members and wondered what the teens were doing on the wharf, as it was now dark with only the full moon lighting up the silhouette of their bodies in the night sky. As she focussed on the team, she saw a flash of light reflecting from the hand of one of the teens appearing in the light of the moon. It looked like a knife. One of the members of the crowd was swinging the knife around while the others were trying to avoid it. As one got nicked, he was disqualified and left the cluster. Now there were four on the wharf. The knife was passed on to the next one in the party and the dangerous game was continued. In the night sky there was one whose body didn't dance as well as the others and it seemed as if he had a limp, as if he had an artificial limb. This was a boy's game, threatening and dodgy. Trish observed the risky game but didn't intrude. Another one was nicked and left the party; then another one met the same fate which left only two on the wharf, the one holding the knife and the boy with the limp. At this point, the boy with the knife should have stopped and the two should have left for home, but they didn't. The boy holding the knife suddenly stabbed the other boy and pushed him off the wharf and into the water. It only took seconds for Trish to realize what had happened and she raced into the water to rescue the boy in the water. She used her life- saving skills to save him. When she got him to the shore, the other Camden Mystery Club members came to help carry him onto the beach and laid him on the sand. They noticed his prosthetic right leg. The teen was seriously injured. The boy mumbled, "Brennan won the game," and died with blood seeping out of his stab wound. Trish immediately took charge. She called 911 for an ambulance to attend to the boy. The Kings District RCMP and an ambulance were on their way. Then she said, "John, text Charlie and tell him it's an emergency and he had better get here now! We've got to handle this situation when the police get here. Did any of you see where the boy who pushed the other boy off the wharf went?"

"I was so preoccupied watching you save the boy I didn't notice," said Josie.

"I thought he left the wharf, but couldn't see which way he went," said Paul.

"John, did Charlie text you back?"

"'He said he was coming," answered John.

Charlie showed up staggering from the effects of the beer he drank. He saw the body of the boy and turned his head and vomited. "You are drunk, Charlie. This is no time to appear plastered when the cops are coming," said Trish. "This boy is dead. He has no pulse and no heartbeat. Shape up, Charlie."

"Sorry, Trish, I was just having a few with my friends."

"I've never seen you like this. What the heck is going on?"

"Lay off, Trish. I'm of legal age to have a drink, but you'll have to drive us home."

Just then the RCMP car and ambulance arrived. The paramedics pronounced the body dead, placed the boy on a stretcher, covered the body, and put it in the EMS ambulance to take to the Queen Elizabeth Hospital in Charlottetown.

The two officers, Corporal Jane Pringle and Constable Jerry Sanders, questioned the Camden Mystery Club members and a few others who came by to see what was happening. They noticed Charlie's drunken behavior and asked if he had a ride home. Trish told them that she would be driving him. The Mounties wanted to know the boy's name. Someone at the beach said his name was Ethan Laird. Then Trish remembered Ethan's last words. She said that Ethan said, "Brennan won the game" which were the last words spoken by the boy. The police told the crowd to clear up their mess, break up and head for home. The park was officially closed for the night.

The police stuck around to make sure all the teenagers left the scene, keeping the contact information for each one. Corporal Pringle and Constable Sanders heard that Brennan was the name of a teen that had a gang following from Colonel Gray High School in Charlottetown, and his last name was Gordon. The detectives jotted this information down; then taped off the wharf where Brennan Gordon stabbed and pushed Ethan Laird into the water.

CHAPTER 2

Trish was very late arriving home and had a tumultuous sleep, dreaming of the scene she had viewed on the wharf. She had never experienced such a horrible game played by kids her own age. She awoke wide-eyed with her heart racing. "Brennan won the game." He survived and killed Ethan. A teenage, daring knife game; was it only a bad dream or was it a premonition? Trish got up and wrote down her dream. It was 4:00 a.m. She decided to stay up; so she quietly dressed and went for a run. She ran around the block and down to Westwood Elementary school. Then she took a trail through the woods and came out near the pond where geese and ducks were still asleep. By the time she arrived back in her neighborhood she had run for over an hour. It was still early. She didn't want to wake up her dad, Staff Sergeant of the RCMP or her brother; so she went to her room and re-read her apparently-realistic dream/premonition.

What would Brennan's motive for stabbing Ethan be? Was he high or just vindictive towards a boy with an artificial leg? And why the heck did Charlie end up drunk at the crime scene?

What a jerk her brother could be. The sky was becoming clearer as the sun appeared over the horizon. Trish heard someone get up; so she decided to take her shower. After she showered and got dressed, she met her dad in the kitchen. "You look as if you've been up for a while, Trish. Did you have a sleepless night?"

"Kind of, I went for a run."

"How was Basin Head? Did everything go OK?" "I witnessed a stabbing and recovered a boy with a prosthetic leg from the water when the killer pushed him off the wharf. That is why we were so late getting home. Constable Jerry Sanders and Corporal Jane Pringle arrived with an ambulance. The body was taken to the QEH."

"My dear daughter, even when you are having fun, you get yourself tangled up in some sort of murder. I think you should let this one go. Let the Kings District RCMP look after things."

"I'm tired and I can't think straight. The detectives have our contact information if they need it."

"Dr. Mack Pathius will be viewing the body this morning. I'll get a report from him. Where's Charlie? He's usually up by now."

Trish wasn't going to rat on her brother's hangover.

She said, "I don't know. It was a late night." "I'm heading out soon. Have a good day." "You have a good day too, Dad."

It wasn't long after Rob left for work that Charlie woke up and met his sister in the kitchen.

"I've got a pounding headache and I feel like crap."

"You've got a hangover and it serves you right. You left the Club to go drinking with your friends and missed seeing a boy, Ethan Laird, murdered last night."

"Oh, shoot! Did Josie, John, and Paul witness it too? Ow. It hurts to talk. I need some water and a Tylenol."

"I actually saw someone stab the boy, but it was dark and I can't be sure of his face. Then I saw the guy push the boy off the wharf and into the water. That's when I went into the water to try and rescue him. John, Josie and Paul were there to help me carry his body to the shore. I shouted to John to text you to come. Ethan's last words were 'Brennan won the game;' then he died right there on the beach. You saw him while we waited for the Mounties."

"I vaguely remember. Didn't he have a fake leg?" "Yeah, it's called a prosthetic leg."

"What happened after that?"

"Geez, Charlie. Don't you remember anything?" "I remember I threw up."

"Yeah, and the RCMP came and it was lucky for you that they didn't take you to jail to sleep off your drunkenness. I told them I'd drive you home and that Rob Camden is our father. They figured that I'd be responsible for your safety and Dad would help me get you into bed if I needed any help."

"Oh, I remember your supporting my weight with your shoulder as you got me out of the car." Charlie got some water and Tylenol and sank into a chair in the kitchen. He laid his head on the table.

"Dad doesn't know about your behaviour last night, but I'm not going to bail you out every time you have too much to drink."

"I'm going back to bed."

"When you get up, take a shower and wash your smelly clothes. You reek of beer."

"Whatever." Charlie rumbled down the stairs to his bedroom and crashed out on his bed.

Trish had her own plans for the day.

CHAPTER 3

Trish worked shift work and so did Josie and John. It was Saturday and Trish had to work the evening shift at Pizza Delight; the twins were to work the afternoon and evening shift at Cows; Paul had weekends off and so did Charlie, but he didn't count as he was nursing a sore head; so the others decided to discuss the events from last night. They met up at John and Josie's house at 10:00 a.m. "Did any of you guys see the Brennan fellow stab Ethan?" asked Trish.

"It was dark, Trish; I may have seen something, but I can't be sure," said Josie.

"I wasn't even sure there was a knife at all. We were quite far from the wharf," said John.

"All I remember was seeing you run into the water and helping you bring the boy, Ethan, to shore," said Paul. "I wasn't paying attention to the game on the wharf."

The two RCMP officers who arrived at the scene got a good description of the victim, Ethan Laird. Teens that were at Basin Head said he went to Colonel Gray High School in Charlottetown, and was friendly and popular with teachers and students alike. Ethan had a positive attitude, didn't do drugs, and didn't drink alcohol. He did well in school, was on the Student Council, and joined other activities at school and in the Charlottetown community. He was well-spoken and presented himself with confidence on a variety of topics and was a member of the War Amps on Prince Edward Island.

Corporal Pringle and Constable Sanders also found out about the gang that the Brennan fellow belonged to. From information they acquired during their initial questioning at Basin Head, they heard there was a gang leader named Brennan Gordon who had several teens that hung around with him. The next day the detectives started their morning by leaving Kings County and going to Charlottetown. First, they went to the RCMP detachment where they met Sergeant Frank Brown and

Corporal Kurt Lewis, who were the detectives working on cases in the Charlottetown area. Corporal Pringle and Constable Sanders transferred their duties to the Charlottetown detachment through the update they provided about the death of Ethan Laird. Frank Brown and Kurt Lewis, from the Charlottetown detachment had several complaints about Brennan Gordon; so, they spoke to their supervisor, Rob Camden, the staff sergeant, who advised them to bring him in for questioning.

CHAPTER 4

The two detectives arrived at the home of Shane and Freda Gordon in Brighton, a subdivision of Charlottetown, looking for their son, Brennan. They went to the front door and rang the bell. An unshaven, overweight, middle-aged man wearing sweat pants and a sweat shirt which didn't cover his entire stomach, answered the door. Seeing a Mountie car in his driveway, he was annoyed. "What do you want?"

"Is Brennan home?" Sergeant Frank Brown asked. "What the heck did he do now?"

"I'm Sergeant Frank Brown and my partner is Corporal Kurt Lewis and we have a few questions for your son. Is he home?"

It was midmorning. The detectives noticed the man's breath had a stench of alcohol. He had a bottle of beer in his hand. Their impression of Brennan's home was repulsive. "He's not here."

"When will he be back?"

"He's eighteen; so who knows. Now go find someone else to harass."

"Does he have a special hangout or friends he hangs around with?" asked Brown.

"Look, He's not here. He didn't come home last night and he could be anywhere. Now go away," said Shane Gordon.

"Please give him my card and ask him to call when he arrives home. We just want to talk to him." Frank Brown passed a card to Brennan's dad and he and Kurt Lewis left.

"That was a waste of time," said Kurt.

"He probably knows more than he's willing to tell us. I don't expect him to give the card to Brennan. Let's head to Tim's for a coffee."

Sergeant Frank Brown and Corporal Kurt Lewis drove to the nearest Tim's and picked up their favourite coffees, swung around the block in the police car, drove around the local schools in the Brighton area, and headed to Victoria Park. "Brennan probably crashed at a friend's house. Read the notes from Corporal Pringle and Constable Sanders to find out the names of some of Brennan's friends that he hangs around with," said Frank.

"There are four names listed here with cell numbers for each. Should we check their whereabouts?"

"We've got to start somewhere. We've got Daniel, Stu, Nick, and Nathan, all friends of Brennan. One of them would know where the heck he is," Frank said perturbed.

Kurt called each of the boys using their cell numbers to see whether they knew where Brennan was. Just by luck, Nathan said he was at his house. Kurt explained that he had some questions about Basin Head from last night and wanted to see Brennan. Could Nathan give him his address? Kurt didn't let on he was a Mountie. Nathan wasn't at Basin Head last night and knew nothing of the situation; so, he agreed to give his address to Kurt who explained how important it was for him to speak with Brennan. When the two detectives arrived at Nathan's house in a police car, Nathan realized he was getting his friend in trouble.

Nathan said, "There are two Mounties coming out of their car looking to speak with you," as he and Brennan peaked out of the window. "Do you know what they want?"

"Yeah. Oh brother, I need to get out of here now. I'm heading out the back door. I'll catch you later." Brennan dashed out the back door as the doorbell rang.

"Good morning," said Sgt. Brown to Nathan. "Is Brennan Gordon here?"

"You just missed him. He's gone."

There was no time for niceties as Brown and Lewis dashed out of the yard to head for the boy on the run. They just got a glimpse of him running through backyards as he tried to escape. The detectives split up and raced after him. Brennan was out of breath and hung over; so he collapsed in the fifth backyard where Brown and Lewis caught up with him, handcuffed him and dragged him back to the police car and shoved him in the backseat. Out of breath, Brown said, "We are taking you to the RCMP headquarters for questioning about a murder last night at Basin Head. You have the right to remain silent but it would be more beneficial if you cooperated."

Brennan said nothing. Sgt. Brown drove the car to the station where the two detectives brought the boy into an interrogation room.

Brennan was a gang leader. He was a big fellow, six feet tall, with half of his head shaved, the other half with black hair, and a beard. He was abrasive, bold and brazen with the cops. He never let his guard down. The Mounties' questions began, "we've heard you were at Basin Head last night. You and some friends were playing a little game on the wharf with a knife. Is that true?"

"No comment," said Brennan.

"We've got a dead body of a boy named Ethan Laird. Do you know anything about that?"

"No comment."

"We have witnesses that have testified you were the one who stabbed Ethan and pushed him off the wharf."

"No comment."

The detectives were exasperated with the teenager. Finally Frank said, "We'll leave you here for awhile until you begin to cooperate."

Frank and Kurt left the room.

CHAPTER 5

Trish sent a text to her dad. *Did the detectives bring Brennan in for questioning?*

She got a message back. Yes.

"Brennan is at the detachment now. What do you want to do guys?" Trish said to the three Club members who were with her.

"I have Ethan Laird's home address on Google. Why don't we visit his family, since the detectives are already questioning Brennan," said Paul.

"That's a good idea. You and I should go together. Josie and John have to get to work this afternoon. Let's drop by for a visit to the family after lunch."

"OK," said Paul. "I'll pick you up at 2:00 p.m. See you later, Trish."

The CMC dispersed. Trish went home for lunch and the twins stayed home to get ready for their work shift at 3:00 p.m.

Paul went to Tim's for a coffee and a snack before he headed home for lunch.

When Trish came home, she was surprised to see Charlie dressed and drinking a beer in the kitchen so early in the day. "You'd better not get addicted to that stuff. You know we have alcohol dependence in our genes on both sides of the family."

"Lay off, Trish. I got drunk last night for the first time and now you think I can't handle a couple of beers. You can be so high and mighty. Mind your own business."

"Well, it's early to start drinking in the morning. Paul and I are going to visit Ethan Laird's family this afternoon. Josie and John have to work today. You're free to do as you please. Just don't get drunk again today. Where did you get the beer? I didn't see any in the fridge."

"I have my own sources."

"It's too bad you are so caught up with alcohol that you will miss out on our investigations."

"I don't have work on the weekends. Dad isn't home either and so I can do as I please. It's hot outside and I'm just quenching my thirst."

"Suit yourself." Trish thought nothing more of her brother. He was a pain at times.

After having a peanut butter and jam sandwich and a glass of ice tea, Trish made a list of questions to ask the Laird family. Paul, who was usually late for CMC meetings arriving with munchies, surprised Trish arriving at 2:00 p.m. with no food. Trish noticed Charlie sitting outside on the deck with a case of beer by his side while reading a mystery novel. She was worried about him but hopped into Paul's parent's car and they headed to Ethan Laird's home which was in Charlottetown. How were they going to explain their visit when they didn't even know the teenager? thought Trish. Paul pulled into the driveway of the Laird residence. The home was a two-storey home decorated with island sand stone, cheery, yellow siding and navy blue shutters adorning the windows. The two of them walked up to the house and Trish rang the doorbell.

The door was answered by a teary-eyed woman in her forties.

"My name is Trish and this is Paul. We were at Basin Head last night and I saw your son, Ethan, being stabbed and thrown off the wharf into the water. I retrieved him from the water and brought him to shore."

"Please, come in." The two teens were ushered into a lovely, decorated living room filled with family members. "My name is Elizabeth, and the people here are my husband, Peter, and our twins, Avery and Andrew." Elizabeth also introduced Trish and Paul to her two brothers, Keith and Kevin, and Peter's sisters, Susan and Louise. She then guided them to the dining room where there was an assortment of food on the table. "Please, help yourselves."

"We wanted to offer our condolences on the death of your son, Ethan," said Trish. "It was such a senseless death. I rushed into the water to get him. When I brought him to shore, his last words were, 'Brennan won the game.' Do you know who the name, Brennan, refers to?"

Elizabeth was caught off guard with this news. "Yes. If I am right, it refers to a boy, Brennan Gordon.

He's a real trouble maker and has had it in for Ethan for a long time. They both go to Colonel Gray High and I don't know why but ever since Ethan got his prosthetic leg Brennan has been a name we've heard a lot."

"What happened to Ethan's leg?" asked Trish.

"It happened a long time ago. Brennan and Ethan were playing near my brother, Keith, who was riding on his lawnmower. They were seven. Keith was there with them and mowing…" Elizabeth's eyes began to tear up; so Keith filled in the rest by saying,

"I was mowing the lawn when the two boys horsed around with a soccer ball and the next thing I knew, the ball was in front of the lawn mower and Brennan and Ethan chased it. Ethan slipped in front of the mower and I accidently ran over his leg. It was mangled; Brennan took off and I called for help.

That's when my wife, Julie, called 911 and an ambulance came and took Ethan to the hospital. There was no way they could save the leg. I think ever since Ethan wore a prosthetic limb Brennan has treated him differently. They used to be friends at age seven but by the time they were teens, Ethan began to excel at his academic work and began to join school activities. He became popular with supportive friends and Brennan was always a leader needing to boast and brag and control friends; he started his own gang and began to belittle Ethan whenever he was near him. They avoided each other in school but Ethan had a huge following on social media and Brennan was jealous of this."

"That's a sad story. Do you know that this Brennan is the same one from Ethan's childhood?" asked Trish.

"Definitely. There is only one Brennan in Ethan's life, Brennan Gordon," said Elizabeth. The whole family sitting in the living room agreed. Paul got up and made his way to the table of food before Kevin said, "Brennan has to pay for his crime. He murdered Ethan."

"I agree," said Peter, Ethan's dad.

"I think the detectives have Brennan at police headquarters for questioning right now," said Trish. "My dad is Rob Camden and he is the Staff Sergeant for the RCMP. I sent him a text and he answered that Brennan is in the interrogation room as we speak."

"Brennan's dad will bail him out. This is a very old story. Brennan gets in trouble with the law and his obnoxious father finds a way to wheedle the law to get his actions acquitted," said Louise.

The others were all in agreement. The mood in the room began to get agitated and tempers began to flare. "He better not get off this time for murder," said Kevin.

"We shall see," said Elizabeth.

"When will the funeral take place?" asked Trish. "The obituary will be in Monday's Guardian and the funeral will be on Thursday," said Peter.

Trish saw Paul with a plate of food. She didn't want anything to eat right now. She wanted to leave the scene of angry, distraught relatives. The family offered her to help herself; so out of courtesy she took a cup of tea and a biscuit. Once Paul was finished, Trish said good-bye and they left. In the car Trish said, "Do you get the impression that Brennan has caused great deal of grief for the Laird family?"

"There were a lot of family members voicing their opinions about Brennan. I wonder whether Sgt. Brown and Cpl. Lewis have made any progress in getting a confession from him."

"Let's head over to the station and see for ourselves," said Trish.

"OK. I won't be surprised if his dad is there bailing him out," said Paul.

"I thought that myself."

The two sleuths parked in the RCMP parking lot area reserved for visitors. They made their way to the front door and asked to see Trish's dad. Rob greeted them with a frown. "What are you doing here?"

"We're checking up with you about Brennan's arrest and if he has confessed?"

"Well, Sgt. Brown and Cpl. Lewis had to release him on circumstantial evidence. There wasn't enough proof to convict him. Some of his friends came and picked him up. Now you had better leave. I'll see you at supper."

"We know he is the killer and Ethan Laird's family can attest to that. Brennan and Ethan have known each other a long time. We'll go, but you'll have a lot of hostile family members of Ethan wanting justice."

"We can't keep him on speculation, Trish. We need proof, such as the murder weapon."

"Paul and I will go. See you later, Dad."

Rob gave a wave to his daughter and Paul and went back to his office.

CHAPTER 6

Brennan was picked up by Daniel Simmonds, Stu Coates, and Nick Lockhart, in Nick's car. They were a tight group of friends and whatever Brennan said was gospel. Brennan led the way and the others followed. Brennan had to dispose of the murder weapon which he had left under the seat in Nick's car last night.

"Nick, take us to Blooming Point. I know a private beach where no one will ever find this weapon," as he pulled the knife out from under the front, passenger seat of the car. Nick followed Brennan's orders.

The gang showed Brennan the nicks they got when he cut them at Basin Head. They were proud of the war wounds. As they got closer to Blooming Point, Brennan directed Nick to take a left, then a right down a red, clay road to an isolated beach. The four of them got out of the car while Brennan buried the knife in a sand dune. They applauded the leader as he did his dirty deed. Brennan felt relief. They were in control of their destiny. The gang headed back to Charlottetown to hang out in the basement of Brennan's parent's house to get out of the heat of the sun where Brennan ruled the household especially with his dad who always came to his side to fight battles for him.

When the boys were in Brennan's room, they played video games and drank beer with his dad. They went out after the sun set to seek trouble. They headed to Victoria Park.

The gang was being followed for the past few days. They weren't sure who was following them but they knew a dark, gray car seemed to find them at one place or another. They were about to vandalize the dairy bar when a tall man dressed in dark clothing with a black, face mask and a gun halted them and pointed the gun at Brennan and pulled the trigger. Within seconds the mystery man and the gang fled leaving Brennan lying in a pool of blood. The masked man disappeared into the night. The boys ran and ended up at Nathan's house. Nathan's parents were home. The boys were hysterical. Nathan said that one of them should call 911. Nathan's father made the call giving the location of the shooting. An ambulance arrived at the scene. No one was there with the body. The EMS attendants brought the boy to the hospital where he was met by a medical team. Brennan Gordon was pronounced dead at 11:24 p.m. The contents of his pockets revealed his ID; i.e., name, date of birth, address, and parents' names. He was only eighteen. Sgt. Brown and Cpl. Lewis were on duty that night. They followed up on the 911 call and proceeded to the hospital.

CHAPTER 7

The day of Ethan Laird's funeral arrived and the Camden Mystery Club was in attendance. The funeral home was packed with family, teachers, parents, and classmates that knew the sad news of the boy with the prosthetic leg. He was such a positive force in the school and community. The CMC took seats at the back of the room. Peter and Elizabeth Laird held each other with tears in their eyes as kind words were spoken about their son. The twelve-year-old twin brother and sister were sitting beside their parents. In the next row were Ethan's uncles, Keith and Kevin and their spouses, and across from them were Peter's sisters, Susan and Louise with their spouses. Monte Pittman, family friend, sat near the CMC in a back row. The eulogy was given by Ethan's Uncle Kevin. Trish kept her premonitions and photographic memory in acute alertness. The reception took place in the funeral home after the service. The CMC mingled and offered condolences to the relations and people who were friends of the family. Trish and Paul had met the family at Peter and Elizabeth's house the day after Ethan was murdered. Now they met some of the aunts and uncles that were relations by marriage. Trish struck up a conversation with Monte Pittman. "Do you live here in Charlottetown, Mr. Pittman?"

"Actually, no. I work for the Maritime Provinces providing prostheses for a company out of Halifax. That is where I live with my wife and children. I have been a family friend ever since Ethan got his first prosthetic leg for which I fitted him. I just arrived to pay my respects to the family as Ethan was such a joyful teenager. He was on his way to making a real contribution to this world and it's so sad he's gone."

Trish got a real sense of grief from Monte Pittman. She excused herself and met up with several family members who were talking about Brennan Gordon. They wanted justice and they riled each other up with talk of Brennan. Trish listened but didn't engage in any further talk. The CMC met up after the reception, briefly shared their insights, and headed back to their homes in Cornwall.

CHAPTER 8

Sgt. Brown and Cpl. Lewis left the hospital and arrived at the home of Shane and Freda Gordon. They notified them of Brennan's death. The detectives said the Gordons should come with them to the hospital morgue to identify the body. Shane and Freda were in shock. They had been drinking and were numb with pain. Shane broke down and wept at the sight of Brennan. Freda wailed. The parents clung to each other in the depths of raw emotion. Brown and Lewis took them back to their home giving them time to recover from the shock, staying with them for an hour or so until they started to settle and begin to make plans for the funeral.

Early the next morning, Rob got a call from Sgt. Brown. He shared the news with Trish. Charlie was hung over for two days in a row and incapacitated, as he was sleeping off the effects of his binge drinking. Rob was ticked off when he found empty beer bottles strewn all over the deck. "How long has this been going on?" he asked Trish.

"Not too long. Charlie had a few too many at Basin Head a week ago. It was the first time I knew he exceeded his limits."

"Why has he started drinking alone? This is not a good sign. I've told you stories of my parents and my alcoholic father. I don't want Charlie to end up like him."

"I know, Dad. I'll keep an eye out for him. Nana had a tough life with Papa, as you told me how he died from drinking too much over the years; his liver gave out in the end."

"You know the story. I hope Charlie isn't starting that habit. It is serious, Trish. Why is he turning to beer now? Is his job too stressful? Is he having girlfriend problems? He doesn't say much about his private life to me anymore. Keep me informed of his drinking, Trish. Now regarding Sgt. Brown's call, Brennan Gordon is dead. He was shot at close range near the dairy bar at Victoria Park last night. I know you'll want to bring your Club together to discuss the murder."

"Yes, I'll text them now." Trish got texts back from Paul, and John and Josie that they were all able to come over that morning. Rob was going to the QEH to see Dr. Mack Pathius and to hear his pathology report on the victim.

The Mystery Club met at the clubhouse in the basement of the Camden home which was decorated with posters representing past, successful murders that they had solved. There was an old record player where the Club played Beach Boys and other records as well as using an old Nintendo and TV. The lighting came from an old lamp that had a flower pattern on the shade which belonged to Trish's nana.

The twins arrived for the meeting at 10:00 a.m. while Paul stopped at Tim's on his way over to pick up a box of Timbits and a coffee. The meeting started with Charlie interrupting the group by coming out of his bedroom and saying, "You've started without me."

Trish was peeved. "We've got things to discuss, dear brother. If you want to join us, then shape up and come and sit down."

"Hang on. I'm coming."

Charlie went to the bathroom, splashed water on his face and then came into the rec. room. Trish started the meeting. "We have two murders to discuss. Ethan Laird was murdered at Basin Head on Friday night and from Paul's and my visit to his family a week ago the cluster of family members was 100 percent sure the killer was Brennan Gordon. Then last night Brennan Gordon was shot and killed at Victoria Park. There was no one there at the scene when the ambulance arrived to pick him up. It looks like a retaliation by Ethan's family, but no one knows for sure. Another thing we have to consider is the fact that Brennan never goes anywhere without his gang members. Once he was shot, they must have run off. Does anyone wish to discuss these murders?"

"Where do we start looking for the killer of Brennan Gordon?" asked Josie.

"That's a good question," said Trish. "We can approach his gang, interview them, and find out who was actually at the murder scene last night."

"We can also question some of Ethan's family members," said Paul. "They were so adamant about Brennan's being Ethan's killer that they must had a strong motive to get even."

"Paul is right," said John. "They may have taken the law into their own hands."

"OK," said Charlie. "I'll stay here and receive any reports by text from you guys. Trish and Paul, you've already gone to see the Laird family and we've already been to Ethan's funeral; so I suggest you two spend some time finding the gang members. John and Josie, you've got a shift at Cows today."

CHAPTER 9

It was another hot, August day and since Charlie was home, he helped himself to some refreshing, cold beer. The more he drank, the more he craved the buzz in his head and the lack of inhibitions he felt. He did have problems, girlfriend problems. He and Josie had been a couple for a short while a couple of years ago; then when he attended UPEI, he dated a girl from one of his sociology classes, Tara MacAskill. He really liked her, but she wanted to play the field and date other guys; so he was just one of several teens she dated. *He didn't like his position, but what could he do?* he thought. The beer numbed his feelings. He didn't get any texts from the Club; so he decided to head to the liquor store to buy some stronger booze besides beer. The old Toyota was in the yard. He grabbed the keys which hung on a hook by the back door and started the car.

The distance wasn't far from his home down the hill to the strip mall where the liquor store was located. He was carelessly driving under the influence of alcohol. He was blurry-eyed, but made it as far as the parking lot when unexpectedly he ran into a parked car in front of the liquor store. The person in the car got out to view the damages. Charlie slurred his words when he said, "I'm soo… ssorry."

The man in the other car noticed a huge dent in his rear fender. It was too much damage to dismiss the incident; besides this boy was drunk. The owner of the damaged car called 911 and demanded that Charlie stay with him until the police arrived.

Charlie was remorseful and apologized through teary-eyes and was frightened that his dad would find out. When the Mounties arrived, Charlie didn't recognize them, but they knew who he was and made him take a breathalyzer test which showed that the alcohol level in his body was twice the legal limit. He was charged with impaired driving and put in the RCMP car. The man whose car was damaged got the information needed for insurance and had his car towed to a local garage. Charlie was taken to the RCMP station at Maypoint and put in a room. The arresting pair of Mounties called their Staff Sergeant, Rob Camden and relayed the message about his son.

Rob Camden had just received the coroner's report from Dr. Mack Pathius when he received the call from the Maypoint detachment. He controlled his emotions, but had to leave the hospital without delay. Pathius knew something was up but wasn't one to pry in other people's business. It was around lunchtime when Rob found his son in the RCMP holding room. Charlie took one look at his father and burst into tears. Rob just stood there allowing Charlie to gain some composure. Finally,

Rob spoke, "Charlie, you've got a criminal record for driving under the influence of alcohol. You have damaged another person's car, your own car, and have had your licence suspended. I can't understand how in heck you did this to yourself. I am thoroughly disappointed in you and I am worried about your ability to drink in moderation. You are exhibiting behaviour of an alcoholic and I won't tolerate it from you. You have a job at UPEI. You must clear your system of alcohol today. I'm taking you home. If you ever become drunk again and I mean ever, you'll be sent to the detox centre in Mount Herbert and will become a member of an Alcoholic Anonymous (AA) group. My father put my mother through hell with his drinking and I will not stand by and see my own son do the same thing. Is that understood?"

"Yes, Dad, I'm so sorry. I really botched things up."

"You'll have to have your insurance company cover the costs of damages to the man's car and to your and Trish's car. You will probably be fined as well and lose your licence for several months Your car has been impounded. I will look at the damages and take the car to a garage to get it fixed so Trish will be able to drive it. Now it's time to go. I'm driving you home."

With tears in his eyes he repeated how sorry he was and said it would never happen again.

Once Charlie and his dad headed to Cornwall, Rob said, "alcohol has been a very sore spot in my memory as a child. My dad was a happy drunk but he tortured my mother with money matters, spending any extra cash on booze. Your nana had years of dragging Dad home from a party or bar. I won't tolerate it with you. You've got your whole life ahead of you, you're smart, and you have a great summer job at the sociology department of the university. You can continue to be involved with the Mystery Club, and you like sports; so let's nip this alcohol dependence in the bud. What do you say?"

Charlie's head was spinning. He just said, "OK, Dad."

CHAPTER 10

Trish and Paul started their gang inquiries at Nathan's house. Trish knew that it was Nathan's house where Brennan had slept on the Friday night after Ethan's murder. She checked with the detectives, Sgt. Brown and Cpl. Lewis. Brown told her they had a chase scene catching Brennan as he fled from Nathan's house. Trish had a better rapport with Frank Brown and Kurt Lewis this year, as they realized the CMC motives and their interest in helping to solve crimes.

Nathan's dad came to the door when Paul and Trish arrived. Nathan's parents knew that he was part of the Brennan gang, and were thankful he wasn't at Basin Head on the Friday night of the killing. They were concerned about the gang showing up last night in panic mode. From what Nathan's dad gathered, the gang witnessed Brennan being shot and the members all fled the scene of the crime and arrived at their home around 11:00 p.m. When Nathan's dad asked the two standing at the door what they wanted, Trish began her spiel. "We are members of the Camden Mystery Club and my name is Trish Camden and this is Paul. We are trying to piece together the killing of

Brennan Gordon last night. Did you see any of Brennan's gang last night?"

Not inviting them in and wary about these two teenagers asking detective questions, Nathan's dad said, "the gang showed up here and were very upset. I phoned 911 for them and relayed what they told me. Once I made the call, all the gang members left except for Nathan who is still in a state of shock and in his room."

"Would it be possible for us to speak with Nathan?

We'd like to get a description of the murderer." "Hang on. I'll see if he's up,"

Trish and Paul stood in the doorway waiting for several minutes. Finally Nathan came to the door. "Dad said you wanted to talk to me about last night. What do you want to know?"

"Can you give us a description of the person shooting your friend, Brennan?"

"He wore dark clothes and a black, face mask. He was tall and pointed his gun and within seconds Brennan was shot. Once Brennan was down, we all got scared and ran off and came here. That's all I know."

"What are the names of the other gang members with you last night? This is important," said Trish. "Daniel Simmonds,

Stu Coates, and Nick Lockhart. They all went to their homes after Dad made the 911 call."

"And what is your last name Nathan?" asked Trish. "Caseley."

"Can you tell us where the others live, Nathan?"

"I wasn't at Basin Head. I don't want to get the others in trouble."

"You won't be getting anyone else in trouble. It's just procedure for us to interview each of you to find out what all of you saw last night, such as, did you see where the killer went after the shooting, or in which direction did he leave?"

"I'm not sure about that. Maybe one of the others might remember. Stu lives around the corner in a white house on the left-hand side and Daniel lives across the street from him in a blue house. Nick lives on Inkerman Blvd. in a sandstone house on the right."

"Thanks for all your help, Nathan. We'll check things out with them. Don't worry, you won't be in trouble. Have a good day. We will find out who killed Brennan," said Trish.

They waved their hands and hopped into Paul's parent's car.

Likewise, the three remaining boys all remembered the dark clothing and black, face mask, and that the person was tall, but they didn't remember which direction the killer went. Stu thought the murderer might have gone behind the dairy bar, but he remembered that the four boys all ended up at Nathan's place and that Nathan's dad called 911. Nathan's dad sent them all home after that.

"I remember Daniel and I headed for home and Nick had a little further to go, but he ran home as fast as he could," said Stu.

"Well, we didn't get much from the boys. I'm having a tingling feeling that there is more to the fact that all the boys ended up at Nathan's place. Why did they go there? Is Nathan's dad more familiar to each of the boys than any other parent? Why didn't Nathan go to Basin Head with the others? Did he know about the plan to kill Ethan and didn't want to be a part of that?" Trish was musing with Paul in the car after finishing their visits. "I think we didn't ask the boys enough about the plans for the Friday night at Basin Head and the murder weapon. I think we should return to each of them to get their stories about the Friday of the murder and what they did all day on the next day. Turn around, Paul and let's check out Nick's place again on Inkerman Blvd."

For the second time, the two CMC detectives went to Nick's. "Sorry to bother you again Nick, but we have a few more questions for you."

"Whatever," said Nick.

"What was the plan for Friday at Basin Head? I saw you playing a game on the wharf with Brennan and your buddies using his knife. Did you know Brennan had it in for Ethan?"

"We were just having a little fun. Ethan was never part of our gang. We just convinced him to take part in our game. Brennan always thought Ethan was such a picture-perfect student, he always said the right things, became very popular with the girls and teachers at Colonel Gray. Geez, he was a flawless schoolboy. Brennan wanted to bring him down a peg or two. I had no idea he was going to stab him," said Nick.

"Where's the knife Brennan used to stab Ethan?" "You'll never find it," said Nick.

"Why do you say that?" asked Paul. "The gang got rid of it."

"How?"

"The three of us that were at Basin Head went with Brennan and he buried it in a sand dune covered with marram grass," he laughed. "I drove them to a secluded beach near Blooming Point."

"You drove the gang to Blooming Point?" asked Trish feeling a premonition coming on.

"I was just the driver. Brennan gave the directions.

Stu and Daniel were with us."

Trish was getting excited. "Could you find that beach again?"

"Oh, sure, but no one goes there."

"If I tell you it is in your best interest to take us to that beach to see if we could find the knife that stabbed Ethan, would you do that?" asked Trish.

"Why would I want to do that?"

"You'd be helping to bring some sense of justice to Ethan's family and you'd be a hero if we ever found the knife. You could bring Stu and Daniel with us if you like. Just think how important you'd be if we found the knife."

"It doesn't matter much now that Brennan is dead. I'll text Stu and Daniel and see if they will go too." He texted: *can't say/ time to make things right/ we need to go to blooming point/* "They are game to go with us," said Nick when he got their texts back.

"We'll go in your car," said Trish.

"You'll have to pay for the gas," said Nick. "That's a deal."

CHAPTER 11

"Would you recognize the spot where Brennan buried the knife?" Trish asked the kids in the back seat as they headed for Blooming Point in Nick's car.

"Maybe, maybe not, we'll see when we get there," said Daniel.

"Do you remember the roads you took?" Trish asked Nick.

"Yeah, but we have a bigger problem. We are being followed," Nick said. "It's the same dark, gray car that we saw last week in Charlottetown."

"Lose him," said Stu. "Speed up."

"Make a couple of turns to get rid of him," said Daniel.

Nick increased his speed; so did the driver of the gray car. Nick turned left; so did their follower. Nick parked on the side of the road. The suspicious motorist drove past them and made an about turn; so he could see what the car of teens was doing.

He was about three telephone poles ahead of them. "What do we do now?" asked Nick.

"He's watching us and we are in a waiting game. He wants us to make the first move," said Trish. "I have an idea. If you know where we are in correlation to the beach we're going to, then if my memory serves me, we can speed past him for about a kilometer, then take a left into a grassy laneway which is hidden from the road and he'll never find us. He'll need to turn around and by the time he catches up, we'll be out of sight. We'll lose him."

"OK, I'll give it a try." Nick revved up the engine and sped off past the gray car, followed Trish's directions and pulled into the grassy laneway she was talking about. By the time the suspect got turned around, the gang in the car saw him drive past them from their vantage point. "We're safe for now."

Paul said, "Did you get the driver's license on the car, Trish?"

"No, Paul. But I know the car was a Honda Accord. We can check into it later. Nick, let's get back on track to finding the beach you were telling me about."

"We are not far from the first dirt road, but we have to backtrack a little. I think we've lost him for now."

It wasn't long before Nick found the clay roads Brennan had taken them on to the deserted beach where the knife was hidden. The dunes were monumental and high with lots of marram grass on them. They had to park the car behind the dunes. The boys got out with Trish and they headed around the sandbanks to the beach. From the beach they couldn't see Nick's car. The three gang members dispersed and studied the shapes of the mounds of sand. Nick had a good memory for detail. He recognized a spot where the marram grass was bent over and with a shout to the others said he'd found the burial place. Trish and Paul followed Nick, Stu, and Daniel up the dune. Nick started digging. He knew it was here somewhere. To his surprise and delight he exposed the knife. Trish said, "Don't touch it! You need surgical gloves so as not to affect the evidence." Trish put on her gloves and tugged the knife out of the sand.

"I'll take that!" shouted the voice of a tall, slim man with a black face mask pointing a gun at Trish. The man was wearing dark clothing. Trish handed over the knife. The group of teenagers were stunned and frightened. Trish composed herself enough to ask, "What do you want with that old knife?"

"You're a smart girl. You should be able to figure that out. Now don't any of you make a move. I've got what I came for." The masked man climbed over the dune and headed for his car. This time Trish saw the dark, gray car as she scrambled up the dune and with her photographic memory she memorized his licence plate. The man drove off leaving the teens on the sand banks.

Nick said, "Who do you think that was? Was he Brennan's killer? Why was he so interested in getting the knife?"

"He needed proof of Ethan's death by finding the knife that was used to stab him," said Trish, but now I have his licence plate number in my head; so I can look into the mysterious man's identity.

CHAPTER 12

Charlie was out-of-control with his binge drinking. He began drinking after work and continued into the night every day and was hung over the next day at work. His supervisor noticed his work slipping and spoke to him about it. "Charlie, I've noticed your work is not up to the high level of standard I expect from you. Is there something going on that you'd like to share with me?"

"I'm sorry, sir. I will do better; I promise."

"Well, if you don't improve your work, I will have to let you go. The fall term starts in a couple of weeks and I need this research done by then. If you can't handle it, I will have to hand it over to someone else."

This was the catalyst that caused Charlie to drink even more. Rob stepped in one night as Charlie was drunk again and said, "that's it for your drinking, Charlie. I'm driving you to the detox centre in Mount Herbert and you will stay there until I know you are on your way to recovery. Once you are fully sober, you will start attending AA meetings. You have no say in the matter. Pack a bag with clothes and a toothbrush. We are heading out there now. I have spoken to your supervisor and he is giving you the rest of the summer off."

Charlie reminded Rob of his father as he looked sheepish and like a little child crying and pleading with his father not to take him to the detox centre. This was tough love and Rob was stern with conviction. Trish knew enough to stay out of the way. Crying, Charlie got his things and Rob removed him from the house and made the drive to Mount Herbert. When Rob dropped him off and got into the car to drive home himself, he broke down and sobbed for his son.

<h1 style="text-align:center">CHAPTER 13</h1>

Trish typed the PEI licence plate number into the Highways Safety Division website and found out the car was a rental from Young's Auto Dealer. She knew her dad was in no mental state to ask any questions about finding out who registered the car at the dealership; so, she asked for help from the RCMP detectives working on the case. Sgt. Brown was her first choice. Before contacting him, she texted the other three members of the CMC to explain what she was doing. They all gave her support by giving their approval. With the CMC backing her, she sent a text to Frank Brown. It said *could you find out who rented the car with PEI licence plate number 134 PF from Young's Car Dealership?* When Frank got the text, he was surprised that Trish Camden was asking for help. He texted her, will try. Why? She texted him back, *that person has the knife as evidence to show who killed Ethan Laird/ has been following Brennan's gang members.* Frank texted, *thanks, Trish.* Sgt. Brown as a rule always took his partner Cpl. Kurt Lewis on police business. Today was no exception. The two detectives left the Maypoint detachment and went to Young's Auto Dealership. They inquired about the person who rented the car with the licence plate that

Trish gave him explaining it was to follow up on an RCMP matter. The service manager looked up the registered name and said it was for Marlene Pierce. She had a Halifax address as her home address and rented the car for two weeks. Brown relayed the news to Trish by text. Trish was stumped. Marlene Pierce? *It was no woman driving that car. It was no woman hijacking the knife from Trish, Paul, and the gang members out at Blooming Point,* Trish thought. *The person renting the car must have used a fake ID. Who rented the car? Why would a woman rent the car and let a man drive it? Something was very perplexing.* Trish sent a text to the Club members to meet at the clubhouse in her basement right away.

Trish missed Charlie's input at the meeting. She missed the old, careful, sincere brother and hoped that he would have a full recovery, but knew it would take time. She explained Charlie's absence to the Club without disclosing where he was exactly. One thing for sure was that the Club members supported each other despite all their problems. Trish was remembering back when Josie and John's dad had his mental breakdown and how everyone kept the information private. They were not a back-biting, gossip group. They took the challenges of life seriously and respected each other. Once the meeting began, Trish explained the dealership had a woman's name on the rental agreement for the gray car, that she rented it for two weeks and gave her home address as one in Halifax. Her name was Marlene Pierce. The Club was puzzled and confused. Paul searched for a Marlene Pierce in Halifax on his computer laptop.

"Well, it looks as if Marlene Pierce is a real person. She lives in Halifax and… are you ready for this… she's married to Monte Pittman!"

CHAPTER 14

"**H**oly cow!" exclaimed Trish. "Monte Pittman is the prosthesis gentleman I spoke with at Ethan's funeral. He had his wife Marlene Pierce rent the car. He said he had three kids. The whole family must be here on Prince Edward Island at some tourist destination. He's the one who has been driving the dark, gray car."

"Why would Monte Pittman want to find the knife that killed Ethan and why would he kill Brennan?" asked Josie.

"Those are very good questions, Josie, and I don't know the answers."

"Just maybe he is in cahoots with some of the hostile family members who wanted to seek justice for Ethan Laird's murder," said John.

"Maybe he wanted to check the DNA on the knife and take the knife to the Halifax Forensics Lab when he goes home, but that doesn't explain why he'd murder Brennan," said Paul.

Trish's premonitions were tingling. "Maybe he didn't kill Brennan. It was dark and maybe he loaned the car to one of Ethan's male family members who used a gun to kill Brennan."

"All we really know is that he is tall and wore dark clothes and a black face mask," said Josie. "Trish is right. We don't know anything more than Monte Pittman's wife rented the car and Monte drove it most of the time. We can't get Brown and Lewis to bring him in on speculation or we'd have our Club banned for having only weak, circumstantial evidence."

"I think we'd better start looking for the dark, gray car," said Trish. If Young's Auto Dealers said that Marlene Pierce rented the car and Monte Pittman has been driving, it we could check when the car is due back at the dealership. We can do this ourselves. I'm game to go and this time I'd like to take John with me. Is everyone in agreement?" The Club members agreed and Trish and John made plans to visit the auto dealership and would report the news back to the others.

Paul and Josie were to stick together; so they occupied the Freeman house for the time being. Barb and Coady were both home and enjoyed having the two teens visit for a while.

Trish and John left the Camden Club house and Trish drove the repaired, old Toyota to Young's Auto Dealers in Charlottetown. Trish spoke to the attendant at the front desk.

"Good morning, Ma'am. We are looking for some information about a car that was rented to a Marlene Pierce. Do you know when that car is due to be returned?"

"It's funny you mention it. That woman brought the car into the lot and returned it this morning. She paid for it and said she was going home and wouldn't need it anymore."

"Can you tell me if she had another car waiting for her?" asked Trish.

"How would I know that? She just passed me the keys and paid for the rental," the woman said. "I didn't ask her if she had another car waiting for her. I presume she had."

"Thank you for your time. We'd better go," said John. John and Trish were stumped. They sent a text to Paul and Josie. Paul texted back/ *maybe the whole family is heading back to Halifax/ Monte taking knife to Halifax Forensics Lab/.*

Trish and John decided to head to the RCMP station to talk to detectives Brown and Lewis. Trish explained, "We found out the car that Marlene Pierce rented was driven by Monte Pittman, her husband. When Paul and I were with Brennan's gang and found the knife that killed Ethan Laird, we were confronted by a tall man wearing dark clothes and a black face mask and he pointed a gun at me and took the knife from us. I think the man must have been Monte Pittman, as he drove a car with Prince Edward island plate number 134 PF which was returned to

Young's Car Dealers this morning. I think he is taking the knife back to the forensics lab in Halifax for DNA analysis."

"Trish, you may be right. We know all forensics analysis is sent to the RCMP station when it is completed; that is, if we request it. I will put an order in for the DNA to be sent to our office directly. Thanks again, Trish. Do you have any other questions or information?" asked Sgt. Brown.

"We've been thinking that maybe Monte was in cahoots with some of Ethan Laird's family members, as they were very distressed and angry about the death of Ethan. Maybe Monte loaned the car to one of them who shot Brennan. We don't know if this is a fact or just a guess."

"It's a good guess, Trish. The family was definitely very upset over the death of Ethan," said Lewis.

"It is up to the RCMP to follow up on your hunches. We will go to the car dealership and check the rental car for gun powder residue," said Sgt. Brown.

Trish and John left the station and headed for Cornwall to meet up with Paul and Josie at the Freeman's home. The Club discussed the case and were aware that the DNA on the knife would go directly to the Maypoint RCMP station. The Mounties would check the car rental for gun powder residue.

CHAPTER 15

Sgt. Frank Brown and his partner Cpl. Kurt Lewis left the headquarters immediately and went directly to Young's Auto Dealers. They produced their badges and requested to inspect the rental car that had arrived from Marlene Pierce earlier that morning. The woman at the office explained that the car hadn't been properly cleaned yet and she led them to it.

Luckily, Frank and Kurt found a light dusting on the passenger seat and again some powder on the passenger side floor mat. They decided to confiscate the floor mat for the time being and take it to Dr. Mack Pathius to see if it matched his findings when he did the autopsy.

Dr. Pathius had found the bullet in the body of Brennan Gordon and had identified the type of gun as a Glock 22. He said this kind of gun could be purchased at a local gun shop. When Brown and Lewis brought the floor mat to him, he studied it and agreed the powder from the floor mat was from the same gun as the bullet.

"This hand gun can be purchased at a store in the Sherwood Business Centre. I'm not sure of its name but hunting and fishing gear is available there. The Sherwood Business Centre isn't that big. I'm sure you'll find it," said Dr. Pathius.

"Thanks, Mack. We are on our way," said Frank.

The two detectives left the lab and headed for Sherwood. They found the shop and met with the owner.

"Yes, I sold this gun type to a few people who belong to a shooting range and like target practice. All guns sold must be registered and I have that information if you need it," said the owner.

"We do need this information," said Sgt. Brown.

"Let me see. I sold this type of gun to one person in the last six months. It was purchased by a man by the name of Peter Laird."

The name Peter Laird meant something to the two detectives. They thanked the owner, got into the police car and left for the court-house.

"We have to get a search warrant for Peter Laird's property," said Sgt. Brown.

"I agree. Hopefully we won't have any red tape in attaining one," said Lewis.

"This may be the break in the case we've been waiting for," said Brown.

They parked on Water Street and entered the court- house. Within an hour the paperwork was done and they took the search warrant to Peter and Elizabeth Laird's home.

They parked the car and proceeded to the front door, rang the doorbell and waited. It wasn't long before someone came to the door. It was a youth of about ten that answered the door.

"Is your mom or dad here?" asked Kurt. "Mom," called Andrew. "It's for you."

Elizabeth came to the door and was surprised to see two Mounties at the door. "May I help you?"

"Yes Ma'am. We have a search warrant for a gun belonging to Peter Laird. Did you know he has a gun?"

"Why, yes. He always goes target shooting at a local shooting range."

"We suspect his gun was used to kill Brennan Gordon."

Elizabeth froze. She began to shake uncontrollably. She sent Andrew into the kitchen with his twin sister, Avery. Then she said, "He always keeps his gun in the garage. You might as well begin your search there."

Frank and Kurt moved towards the garage door. They entered and began their search. As Mrs. Laird said, they found the gun. It was not in his target shooting bag, but hidden in a pile of hiking gear and shoved into an old boot. They also found a black face mask. They retrieved the two items and put them in the trunk of the car. While they were searching, Elizabeth called her husband at his office and explained frantically what was taking place. He tried to calm her down and said he'd be home within the hour.

The detectives came back to the front door which Elizabeth answered right away.

"I called Peter and he said he'd be home within an hour. You may wish to come back or wait here for him."

"We'll wait in the car, thanks," said Brown.

Did Peter kill Brennan? she thought.

CHAPTER 16

Peter Laird pulled into the driveway to meet the two Mounties getting out of their car.

"Peter Laird?" He nodded.

"You are under arrest for the murder of Brennan Gordon." Kurt handcuffed him and put him in the back seat of the RCMP car. Elizabeth watched from the window.

"Anything you say may be held against you. You have the right to remain silent. You may have one phone call," said Brown.

They took him to the RCMP detachment and left him in an interrogation room. Rob Camden was there and he sent a text to Trish, *FYI Peter Laird is in custody for the murder of Brennan Gordon.* Trish called her dad immediately to get further information.

Trish remembered Peter as being tall and slim at Ethan's parent's home the day she and Paul went to see the family. Peter was Ethan's dad. Monte Pittman was tall and slim as well. He wanted the knife that killed Ethan to prove Brennan had stabbed Ethan. Peter decided to seek justice on his own by shooting Brennan Gordon, who killed his own son.

Trish sent texts to her Club members to meet at the Clubhouse as soon as possible. The Freeman twins and Paul arrived shortly.

"I want to share the news that my dad sent by text after I followed up with him by phone today," said Trish, "but I want all of us to be together to hear the news. Peter Laird is in custody for the murder of Brennan Gordon."

"Wow!" said Paul.

"I can hardly believe it," said John. "I'm shocked!" said Josie.

"It caught me off guard myself. Too bad Charlie isn't here to hear the news. We have lots of loose ends to deal with," said Trish. "I checked with Dad and he said that Peter Laird was fingerprinted and his photo was taken. I'm wondering if the gun which was pointed at me at Blooming Point and the gun shot to kill Brennan Gordon is the same gun or not. I have a good visual memory of the gun pointed at my head; so we could find out through Dad, who could check with Brown and Lewis where Peter purchased the gun. We could go there to identify whether or not it is the same gun. If it is one and the same, we'll have Monte as an accomplice to the murder of Brennan Gordon."

"How do you figure that out, Trish?" asked Josie.

"I think I'm getting ahead of myself. The dark, gray car that Marlene Pierce rented and which Monte Pittman drove to Blooming Point was the same car that Peter Laird used the night Brennan was killed. The detectives checked that the gun powder residue on the floor mat matched the bullet type that came from the Glock 22 according to Dr. Mack Pathius. I got this information when I called my dad when he texted me about having Peter Laird in custody."

So you're saying if we go to the store that sold the Glock 22 to Peter Laird and you identify it as the same gun that Monte pointed at you out at Blooming Point, then you're saying the gun is one and the same. Couldn't there be more than one Glock 22 gun?" asked Paul.

"That's what we have to find out. It's highly unlikely two guns were sold that were one and the same. My premonitions tell me that the two men used the same gun. Remember Monte was a good friend of the Laird family, as he looked after Ethan's prosthesis as Ethan got older and he had a professional relationship with them."

"Why don't we check Google to see if you can identify the gun type used at Blooming Point, Trish?" asked Paul.

"That's a good idea, Paul."

"Here's a picture of a Glock 22, Trish," as Paul showed her the picture on his laptop.

"That's it!" cried Trish. "It's the same gun! I'm going to text Dad and see if Brown and Lewis went to the gun shop and found the gun registered to Peter Laird."

Her dad sent off a text confirming the store sold a Glock 22 to Peter Laird within the last six months. He also sent a text to Trish saying Monte Pittman had just taken the murder weapon for Ethan's death, the knife, into the Halifax Forensics Lab to get DNA analysis done on it. The RCMP in Halifax arrested him on the spot and is holding him in a cell there. They fingerprinted him and took his photo as a preliminary procedure.

"Geez, Trish. The detectives are doing their job," said John. "They know no average person comes into the forensics lab looking for DNA analysis. They were expecting him, weren't they?"

"Yes. They were anticipating his arrival."

CHAPTER 17

Charlie had been in the detox centre at Mount Herbert for ten days when Rob went to pick him up. Rob asked Charlie on the way home about his stay at the centre.

"You'll never see me back there again, Dad. It was terrible. I'll never drink alcohol again. The counsellors recommended I start going to AA meetings. They suggested one in Cornwall within walking distance from home."

"That's a very good idea, Charlie. You'll be back in university and surrounded by temptation and AA meetings can be very beneficial. I will support you in any way that I can, but the work of recovery has to come from you. Alcoholism is like a disease you have to manage."

"I've already been told that, Dad. I promise you I'll never drink ever."

"I'm proud of you, son."

The rest of the way home they drove in silence, both reflecting on the changes that they had to make in their lives. When they got to the driveway, Rob said, "Trish is looking forward to your coming home. She has lots to tell you about the Mystery Club."

"OK. That's good."

Trish hugged her brother when he entered the bungalow. She felt a change in Charlie as soon as she hugged him. Was he able to share his experience or was it so deep that she'd never hear about it? "I'm glad you are home, Charlie. I've missed you."

"I missed you too, Trish. It's good to be home."

"When you are ready to hear the Club news, I have lots to tell you."

"Maybe tomorrow. I just want to settle in here again," he said.

"OK."

Charlie went to his room. He checked out his belongings and noticed his cell phone was on his bedside table. He wasn't ready to text anyone. He thought of Tara MacAskill. He had spoken about her to the counsellor assigned to him at the Centre. He really cared for her, but now he had to get on with his life and she wasn't the one for him. He spent the last ten days searching for the goal he had set for himself when he and Trish started playing mystery games with Dad. He knew deep down he wanted to become an RCMP officer like his dad. He also knew he had to focus on his academic life so he could graduate and apply for RCMP training. He took out the card from his wallet that was given to him on his departure from the detox centre. It said, "GOD grant me the SERENITY to accept the things I cannot change, the COURAGE to change the things I can, and the WISDOM to know the difference. The Serenity Prayer." On the other side of the card was the list of AA meetings with days of the week and times of meetings in various locations on Prince Edward Island. He felt an inner strength in this prayer. He knew at some point he would talk to his sister, but not tonight. Tonight, he would lie in bed and thank God for his blessings.

CHAPTER 18

Staff Sergeant Rob Camden sent Sergeant Frank Brown and Corporal Kurt Lewis to Halifax to bring Monte Pittman back to Charlottetown from the RCMP detachment in Halifax, Nova Scotia. When Monte arrived at the forensics lab, he gave the knife to the RCMP in Halifax in the hope that the DNA would match with a file the RCMP had in Charlottetown on Brennan Gordon. He was detained in a holding cell for hours. Sgt. Brown and Cpl. Lewis arrived and explained to Monte that he was to appear at a hearing in Charlottetown because he was being charged as an accomplice in Brennan Gordon's death. During the drive back to Charlottetown Monte was outspoken. "I didn't have anything to do with Brennan's death. I am innocent. I just wanted to confirm Brennan's DNA with the file on him in Charlottetown and I thought I was being helpful to the RCMP by taking the murder weapon to the Halifax Forensics Lab. I didn't want to wait for the Charlottetown Mounties to delay sending the evidence by using the mail system. I was just trying to speed up the whole process."

"That isn't the way things work in the real world, Monte. You may choose to remain silent and anything you say can or will be used to convict you in a criminal court. Save it for the judge, Monte."

Monte was getting riled up, but knew he might only be providing more evidence against himself; so he remained silent for the rest of the trip. Once the detectives crossed the Confederation Bridge, he realized he would need a lawyer from Prince Edward Island. He had been to the island enough times as a prosthetic technician that he knew the name of a lawyer that he could call.

Frank and Kurt brought him to the RCMP station and put him in a holding cell. They allowed him to make his one call and he asked Eliza Lark to represent him at a hearing which was scheduled for the following week.

Peter Laird needed a legal representative as well and his hearing was scheduled for the day before Monte's hearing. The lawyer representing Peter was Alexander Milner.

The Glock 22 gun had fingerprints of Peter Laird and Monte Pittman on it matching the database information from the RCMP stations. The evidence was convincing. Both men were to appear before two different judges the following week. The main reason for the hearings was to discover if there was enough evidence to charge the accused for a crime; if so, then Monte and Peter would have to go to trial before a jury. Once the preliminary hearing was decided by the judge, the Mounties could follow up with the evidence to proceed with the trial.

The black face mask was an integral part of the DNA analysis data.

Peter Laird's preliminary hearing was conducted before a judge by the name of Gerald Mann. Alexander Milner stated that Peter Laird had no previous convictions. He pleaded not guilty to the murder of Brennan Gordon. However, the judge thought the evidence was enough to support a trial by jury and set a trial date for November 24, 2021. Peter was to appear on that date, but wasn't kept in jail, since this was his first offence and the jails were overloaded at this time.

Monte Pittman's preliminary hearing was held with judge Michael Harris. Eliza Lark made her statement that the evidence on Monte Pittman was sketchy; he held the gun, but didn't shoot it, he wore a face mask, he took a knife from a gang of kids and wanted to have DNA analysis done on it, he followed a group of teenagers around in a rental car, and gave the gray car to Peter to drive on the night of the murder. The judge thought there was enough information for Monte to have a trial for aiding and abetting. His trial was to be held on November 23, 2021, the day before Peter Laird's trial. This gave the detectives and lawyers time to gather information to support their cases.

Brennan's gang, Daniel, Stu, Nick, and Nathan decided to take the law into their own hands.

"Peter Laird needs to pay for shooting Brennan," said Nick.

"Yeah, what do you want to do?" asked Stu.

"Let's wait until dark and do a job on his car," said Daniel.

"Are you with us, Nathan?" "Sure."

The bad boys collected items of food from the kitchens of their parents and headed out at 11:00 p.m. They broke eggs, poured molasses, ketchup, flour, oatmeal, etc. on Peter's car in the driveway. Once they were in the mood for destruction, they slashed his tires, and then ran off.

"We sure did a number on Peter's car," Nick laughed.

"Yeah, did anyone take a picture?" asked Stu.

"I did," said Nathan. He showed the gang the picture of Peter Laird's car on his phone.

"Cool." "Way to go."

"Awesome job," said another.

That was a real getting even, dirty job. The bad boys discussed plans to attend the trial where they would create a raucous, rowdy noise in the court room.

CHAPTER 19

Charlie began attending Alcoholic Anonymous (AA) meetings regularly. The university year started and he had a full course load. He had talked to Trish about his disease and warned her never to have the same thing happen to her. Trish and the rest of the Mystery Club members were back in high school. Charlie rejoined the Club and admitted that he was going to AA meetings regularly and had the support of his long-lasting group of friends. Paul, John, and Josie all welcomed him back into the Club and praised him for his strength to overcome his addiction.

Trish heard about the night of mischief concerning Peter Laird's car. She imagined that it was the gang of boys that wanted to get even. No one was charged, but the RCMP detectives interviewed some of Brennan's old gang. They all lied about their whereabouts on the night of the incident and the Mounties had no proof to substantiate any charges.

Trish kept informed about the data collected by the detectives at the RCMP station. The DNA from the black mask came back and it was found that Peter Laird and Monte Pittman had used the same mask. They were friends and shared not only the mask and the gun, but also the rented car.

The CMC was back in study mode at school. Exams were held and the dates of the trials were coming up. Trish was to testify at Monte Pittman's trial. The bad boys were to testify at Peter Laird's trial. The night before Monte's trial, Trish had a dream of the gun being pointed at her head and then she awoke in a cold sweat. Trish had been in courtrooms before, but never had to testify. She was nervous. She tried to get back to sleep, but only dozed lightly.

Rob was in the kitchen for breakfast when Trish appeared from her bedroom. "Did you get any sleep, Trish? You look tired."

"I couldn't settle my mind. I was thinking about the trial of Monte Pittman today."

"Remember, all you have to do is tell the truth. I thought I'd taught you better than this, Trish. Trials are all about whose truth is more believable to the jury. You have been criminal detectives with your Mystery Club for a few years. You've got this, Trish. Now go take a shower and get ready for the day."

Charlie came into the kitchen. He overheard his sister's worries. He put his arm around her and said, "You are the backbone of the Camden Mystery Club. You will do us proud.

I'm sorry I'll have to miss this trial, but I know you'll do an excellent job."

Trish felt the positive vibes of her dad and brother. They gave her inner strength. "Thanks, you two. I'll go take my shower and get ready for the day."

The courtroom was full. The Laird family took up a large portion of the courtroom also attending were Monte's wife, Trish, Paul, Josie, John, the bad boys, Sgt. Frank Brown, and Cpl. Kurt Lewis, and several other friends and clients of Monte's island prosthetic business.

Monte and his lawyer, Eliza Lark, were seated at a table in front of the crowd. The prosecutor, MacKenzie Pathius, was seated with Shane Gordon, Brennan's dad. The jury entered the courtroom. The clerk of the courtroom said, "Honourable Judge, Michael Harris, all rise."

The judge said, "court's in session." Everyone sat down. MacKenzie Pathius called his first witness, Trish Camden, to the stand. Trish took the oath to tell the truth and sat in the witness chair beside the judge. MacKenzie Pathius asked Trish to describe to the court the night at Basin Head on August 6th exactly as she remembered it.

"My friends and I were having a campfire on the beach at Basin Head when I noticed a gang of teenage boys playing a game on the wharf. One of the boys had something sharp in his hand and waved it around the group of boys and tried to cut them. Once a boy was nicked with the knife he was to leave the game. This happened with each of the boys until there were only two left, the boy with the knife and the boy with the limp. Then almost instantaneously, the boy with the knife stabbed the boy with the limp and pushed him off the wharf and into the water. I immediately rushed into the water and rescued the boy. When I brought him to shore, I was helped by some of my friends. He had a prosthetic leg and was bleeding heavily. The boy said, 'Brennan won the game,' which were his last words. He then died right in front of us. I called 911 and an ambulance and two RCMP officers arrived at the scene within fifteen minutes."

The judge, Michael Harris, said, "Does the defence call any witnesses?"

"No, your honour, the defense rests," said Eliza Lark.

Trish stepped down from the witness stand. Then MacKenzie Pathius called Nick Lockhart to the stand.

Nick was nervous. He went through the courtroom procedures and sat in front of the jury in the witness cubicle. MacKenzie said, "Were you one of the boys playing the game with Brennan the night of Ethan Laird's death?"

"Yes."

"Can you describe to the courtroom the weapon Brennan used in the game you were playing?"

"Yes. It was a knife."

"Can you tell me what happened to the knife after Ethan was stabbed and the game was over?" asked MacKenzie.

"The next day I drove Brennan and two other boys out to Blooming Point and Brennan buried the knife on a secluded beach."

"What happened to the knife then?"

"It was left in a sand dune until Trish Camden, her friend, Paul, and two of my friends went to the beach to retrieve it, but just after finding it, a man wearing a black-hooded face mask pointed a gun at Trish and took the knife. He had been following us and we thought we lost him, but he arrived and took the knife at gun point."

"Your two friends, what are their names?" "Daniel Simmonds and Stu Coates."

"Are they here in the courtroom today?" "Yes."

"Can they prove your story?" "Yes."

"No further questions, your Honour."

Eliza Lark stood up and requested Monte Pittman to take the stand.

Monte moved to the witness stand, took the oath to tell the truth, and took his seat in the witness box.

"Did you point a gun at Trish Camden and take the knife from her?" asked Eliza Lark.

"Yes."

"Did you also follow the teenagers in a dark, gray car?"

"Yes."

"Tell me, what is your relationship with Peter Laird?"

"I am a prosthetic technician and I always looked after Ethan's prosthesis up until he died. Peter Laird was Ethan's dad and we became friends through my relationship with Ethan."

"Did you and Peter share any items?"

"We shared the same black, face mask, the same gun, and the same rental car."

"Did you ever fire the gun?"

"No. I only used it to scare the kids."

"You do realize the jury has witnessed your involvement with Peter Laird and his trial is scheduled for tomorrow. That is all the questions I have at this time, your Honour. I'd like to call Sgt. Frank Brown to the witness stand."

Sgt. Frank Brown stepped up as Monte returned to his seat. He took his oath and sat in the witness box.

Eliza Lark began her questioning. "What happened to the knife that was used to kill Ethan Laird?"

"Monte Pittman took the knife to the Halifax forensics lab to have DNA testing done on it. It isn't protocol for a civilian to make such a request and Monte was detained in Halifax until my partner, Cpl. Kurt Lewis, and I left Charlottetown and went to Halifax to bring Monte back to Prince Edward Island for criminal charges. The knife was checked for DNA and it matched Brennan Gordon's DNA from his clothing which we retrieved from his body after the murder."

"I have no further questions, your Honour," said Eliza.

The prosecution and defence each offered a closing argument of the trial.

The judge said, "Today's session is adjourned until tomorrow at 10:00 a.m. The jury will get together to discuss the verdict."

The groups of people leaving the courtroom spoke in hushed tones. Josie said, "Trish made a good report of the events at Basin Head. Nathan, a member of the Bad Boys, wasn't at Basin Head and didn't go to Blooming Point, but he was glad he wasn't involved in any way with the knife game."

The CMC headed for Cornwall in Paul's parent's car. "Charlie and Dad will want to hear about the trial," said Trish.

Paul dropped the Club members off. Trish wanted to talk to her dad and Charlie about the events of the day. Rob and Charlie arrived home for supper which Trish prepared.

"How was your day?" asked Charlie.

"All went well. I said my piece, Nick Lockhart was called to the stand, Monte Pittman confessed to wearing the same face mask, using the same gun, and using the same rental car as Peter Laird. Sgt. Brown stated that the DNA on the knife was Brennan's. The trial was adjourned until tomorrow at 10:00 a.m."

"I'm sorry I had classes all day and I had just enough time to eat before I went to my AA meeting."

"Glad to hear all went well, Trish," said Dad.

"We shall see tomorrow what the verdict is. Let's eat the tuna burgers I made before Charlie's meeting."

The three of them ate while Trish babbled about the courtroom experience. Rob watched the news, Charlie went to his meeting, and Trish read a mystery novel. That night Trish slept soundly for the first time in months. The alarm went off at 6:30 a.m. She was ready for another day in court. She hoped her teachers wouldn't mind her absence from school.

At 10:00 a.m., the jury arrived in the courtroom. The verdict was guilty by unanimous vote. Monte Pittman was charged with aiding and abetting the murder of Brennan Gordon. The judge declared that Monte Pittman would receive a sentence of five years in Renous Penitentiary.

CHAPTER 20

The trial for Peter Laird began at 2:00 p.m. that day, November 24, 2021. Gerald Mann was the judge presiding over the events of the trial. Alexander Milner was Peter's lawyer and MacKenzie Pathius was the prosecutor. Peter pleaded not guilty to murder.

The courtroom was full once again. The Bad Boys were all in attendance, as well as the Laird family, Shane Gordon, Trish and her Club except for Charlie who couldn't miss classes, Sgt. Frank Brown and Cpl. Kurt Lewis and Dr. Mack Pathius, the coroner.

MacKenzie started the proceedings. "Yesterday we found out that Peter Laird's DNA was on the black face mask used by Monte Pittman. Today we can see why that DNA is significant. We also found out that Peter Laird's DNA was found on the gun, as well as his fingerprints on the rental car used by Monte Pittman. Today this evidence is noteworthy. Who fired the gun that shot Brennan Gordon? I'd like to call Nathan Caseley to the stand."

Nathan's dad was seated in the back of the courtroom. Nathan took the stand and appeared very worried.

"Nathan, please tell the court what happened the night Brennan was shot," MacKenzie began.

"The Gang and I had been playing video games at Brennan's house and when it got dark, we thought we'd hang out around the dairy bar in Victoria Park," said Nathan.

"What time was that?" asked the prosecutor. "It was about 10:30 p.m."

"Go on."

"We were just there at the dairy bar when a tall man wearing a black face mask and dark clothing came out of nowhere and pulled out a gun and shot Brennan."

"Did you see the car he was driving?"

"No. We got scared and took off and ran to my parent's house. My dad tried to calm us down and he called 911 for us. We were pretty messed up. My dad sent the boys home around 11:00 p.m. I couldn't sleep. I lay down but the image of Brennan in my mind kept me awake."

"Thank you, Nathan. You may step down. I'd like to call Dr. Mack Pathius to the stand."

Mack took the stand. He knew why his brother wanted his testimony and he was prepared for it.

"When you did the autopsy on Brennan Laird, can you tell the jury what you found?"

"The bullet I removed from the body was from a Glock 22 gun," said Dr. Pathius.

"Is the Glock 22 a common gun found on Prince Edward Island?"

"It's not uncommon but is usually used for target shooting."

"That is all, Mack. Thank you. I'd like to call Elizabeth Laird to the stand."

Elizabeth Laird was terrified. Things didn't look good for her husband. She took the oath and sat in the witness chair.

"Can you please tell the jury what kind of gun your husband uses for target shooting?" asked MacKenzie.

"Peter has a Glock 22."

"No further questions for this witness. I'd now like to call Sgt. Frank Brown to the stand."

Sgt. Brown took his place in the witness box. "Can you tell me what you found out about the car you found at Young's Auto Dealers?"

"Monte Pittman's wife, Marlene Pierce, rented a gray car from Young's Auto Dealers which was used by Monte on the Island. The car was returned to the dealership the day after the murder of Brennan Gordon. My partner and I found gun powder residue on the floor mat on the front passenger side and took the mat to the RCMP station to determine what kind of gun would create the residue. We sent the sample of residue to the Halifax forensics lab and the result was the gun powder from a Glock 22."

"Can you also tell the jury about the Glock 22 you have at the RCMP station?"

"Yes, we have the murder weapon. The Glock 22 we have in our possession had Peter Laird's and Monte

Pittman's fingerprints on it. We found it and the black face mask in Peter Laird's garage."

It was time for the closing statements. Alexander Milner got up and spoke. "Peter Laird is a law-abiding citizen. He is a teacher at Charlottetown Rural High School with an excellent record. He has never had a criminal record. He lost his son, Ethan, tragically by a gang member, Brennan Gordon, who stabbed him after dark at Basin Head. Peter was emotionally distraught and devastated by his son's death. I want the jury to remember how difficult it is to lose a son or daughter. It is heart-wrenching."

It was MacKenzie's turn to speak. "You've heard the evidence presented to you today. Peter Laird took the law into his own hands and shot Brennan Gordon with a Glock 22. He wore a black face mask which has his DNA on it; the gun used in the murder, a Glock 22, was found in his garage while the bullet in Brennan's body came from that type of gun. The gun residue on the floor mat of the car matched that of the gun used in the murder. Monte Pittman gave testimony yesterday that he and Peter drove the same car. Peter's fingerprints were found on the steering wheel. He is guilty of murder of an eighteen-year-old boy. "

The judge said, "The trial is adjourned until the jury comes back with a verdict." The jury got up and left the courtroom. The judge went to his chambers. The crowd got up and wondered when the verdict would be announced. A half hour passed when the clerk of the trial called the group back into the courtroom as the jury was prepared to give the verdict.

Everyone returned to their seats. The judge and jury resumed their places. The judge asked for the verdict.

"The jury finds Peter Laird guilty in the first degree."

The judge pronounced a sentence of ten years in the Renous Penitentiary.

The Laird family got up and booed. The Bad Boys cheered. There was pandemonium in the courtroom. The Camden

Mystery Club sat and looked shocked at the uproar. Security guards took Peter out the side door; then they returned to seize those who were causing the uproar and took them outside and released them. Order was restored and the trial was over.

EPILOGUE

Ten years later

Staff Sergeant Rob Camden** married **Nora Burns**, a nurse who had cared for him when he had his heart attack.

The Camden Mystery Club

Trish Camden completed a degree in law and took a position in Charlottetown with a legal firm.

John Freeman graduated from UPEI in education and after five years of substituting got a teaching position at Charlottetown Rural High School, teaching math and science. **Trish** and **John** got married.

Charlie Camden graduated from UPEI with an honours B.A. degree and became an RCMP officer in Nova Scotia where he lives with his wife, **Julie Hanahan**, who is a social worker.

Josie Freeman went to Holland College and took a course in Early Childhood Education.

Paul's last name was never revealed until now. His last name is **Dahl** and he is a descendant of **Roald Dahl,** the author's favourite children's writer. **Paul Dahl** is a life-long member of Weight Watchers and lost fifty pounds before he asked **Josie** to marry him. They have a baby on the way. **Paul** got a degree in computer science and creates computer games.